THE PRIMORDIAL TIDE

THE PRIMORDIAL TIDE

Jeffrey Stettler

iUniverse, Inc.
Bloomington

The Primordial Tide

iUniverse books may be ordered through booksellers or by contacting:

iUniverse
1663 Liberty Drive
Bloomington, IN 47403
www.iuniverse.com
1-800-Authors (1-800-288-4677)

ISBN: 978-1-4502-9397-6 (sc)
ISBN: 978-1-4502-9396-9 (dj)
ISBN: 978-1-4502-9395-2 (ebk)

Library of Congress Control Number: 2011906660

Printed in the United States of America

iUniverse rev. date: 06/06/2011

***** PART ONE *****

Chapter 1 - May 12, 2010 – 3:30 PM

Werner G. Straus was an expert organic chemist. He could be a bit eccentric at times, but nonetheless, he was about the best investigative chemist GG Oil Company had. Werner was nearing 70 years old and had already had two heart attacks, the second of which was a near fatal one a year ago. Medication and artery stents now had him nearly back to his normal routine.

Werner was a lonely man. His wife had died of cancer several years ago, and they'd never had any children. His last living relative, a nephew, was killed in an automobile accident last year.

Werner had just returned to work in April, and was assigned to light duty and moved to 2nd shift to minimize stress. His life was his work. He was getting bored and becoming anxious to get some interesting work like the good old days.

Werner's thoughts were interrupted by the department manager Ron Strong, who usually stayed clear of the lab because of alleged chemical allergies, rushing through the doorway with a concerned look on his face. Ron walked hurriedly over to Werner and said, "Werner. I hate to ask this, but I have a #1 priority job for you tonight. We were going to ask Charley to stay over, but he had a family emergency come up."

Werner replied with a grin, "I'm fine, Ron. Besides, I need a little excitement to brighten things up. What do you have?"

Ron handed Werner a large carton with **"Warning Hazardous Material Special Handling Required"** labels all over it. Ron stated emphatically, "These are crude oil samples from the Deep Horizon oil leak in the Gulf. They were flown in late this afternoon. There are different samples taken at various locations. Some were taken by the robot sampler at about 100 feet above the ocean floor because they couldn't get any closer due to the high pressure and turbulence where the leak is. There are also samples taken at 2500 feet above the ocean floor and at the surface. Finally, there are samples from the oil plume about three miles from the leak site, both before and after being sprayed with the Triple D dispersal agent. What we want to know is whether the crude is reacting at all with the salt water and whether the Triple D is doing any good."

Werner asked curiously, "Do you think this crude would react any different from any other crude?"

Ron answered, "No, not really. I heard the core samples near the wellhead were a little weird, but I haven't seen the report so I don't really know the details. I wouldn't want that analysis to bias your results anyway. Because this is the deepest well ever drilled, this may be the oldest oil we've ever recovered. It could be from a period in the earth's history we've never examined before."

"But listen, Werner," Ron said, wanting to get the conversation back to the job at hand, "the thing I need you to accomplish before you go home is to run a batch evaluation of a new dispersing agent called OxiMax #7. This chemical is some secret military brew that may oxidize and break down the oil before it gets anywhere close to land. We don't want word of this getting out because if the media gets wind of it and then it doesn't work, we'll catch a firestorm of bad press. I verified you still have a top secret clearance, so you're ok to work this. The test protocol is in the folder inside the box. They'd like to spray this stuff tomorrow morning if the test results are positive. Unless I hear something from you to the contrary, we'll proceed with the spraying as scheduled."

Werner grinned and motioned toward a good looking young man seated at the corner desk on the other side of the lab. "What about my side-kick Timmy?" he asked.

"I'm going to request he cool his heels tonight and leave you alone. That's something I'm sure he's good at," Ron added sarcastically.

For the last month Werner was teamed with a 22-year-old chemical engineer named Tim Gardner. Tim was just out of college, and rumor had it some high up relative had pulled strings to get him hired. Tim spent more time on his cell phone trying to establish himself as a "Don Juan" than learning the job. This annoyed Werner to no end, plus he kept calling Werner "Gramps" with a fake-looking smile on his face. Werner noted Ron giving Tim his marching orders and thought to himself that this shift was going to be a pleasant surprise. At least he was half right.

Chapter 2 - May 12, 2010 – 5:00 PM

Werner opened the carton carefully and photographed the condition and labels on all the specimen bottles for documentation. Although not required by the specified protocol, he decided to do all testing in the decontamination chamber. He was more concerned about the OxiMax #7 chemical than the crude oil. As he suspected, there were no Material Safety Data Sheets on the chemical, so he didn't know what it was made of, nor if any special handling was required. Consequently, he opted to play it ultraconservative.

Most of the tests on the crude oil were pretty routine, such as density, cracking temperature, ash content, volatility, and water absorption. Since the big boss wanted results of the effect of the OxiMax, he decided to work that first, then follow-up with the rest of the testing, probably tomorrow.

Werner divided up the samples into separate glass test tubes, carefully labeling each with the appropriate code number. He ran a spectral analysis on each sample of the crude oil from each of the various depths. They were all pretty much the same with basic hydrocarbons found in other crude oils. There were some unusual trace elements not normally found in crude oil, but again, this oil was formed from a period of the earth's history not analyzed before. Werner noted this for his report.

Werner then began adding various concentrations of the OxiMax #7 mystery chemical to separate samples of the crude. He usually ran the samples in triplicate to verify repeatability if anything unusual occurred. He kept two crude oil only samples at each depth for a batch baseline. The protocol called for a mild agitation after adding OxiMax to replicate wind and wave action that would mix the chemical into the crude oil. Without telling Tim what it was for, Werner had him set up a shaker table and make the coded labels. This seemed to annoy Tim because it took him away from his cell phone calls to various girlfriends. Werner was really enjoying the moment.

By 6PM Werner completed a 10-minute mild agitation of each of the samples and was about to begin his microscopic evaluation. He was interrupted by the phone, which was his communication from the decontamination lab to the outer lab where Tim was working. Werner answered, "Yes?"

Tim's voice on the phone had his usual sarcastic tone asking, "Hey Gramps, I was thinking of picking up some pizza for our lunch time. Do you want me to bring you back some?"

With all the activity, Werner had lost track of time, but he always brought his own food, which Tim knew full well. He answered, "No thanks. I'll be tied up in here with these samples so I'll probably skip lunch for now. Take your time." Werner felt sure pizza wasn't the only thing Tim would be trying to pick up.

Werner was right. Tim had planned to meet a girl named Tina. He thought she might be under age, but she was really hot which made it worth the risk. Better still, she thought Tim was cool. So Tim figured with a couple of hours to spend, he might even be able to score. After all, his mentor told him to take his time, which he planned on doing anyway. Tim bounded out of the lab and headed for his car.

Chapter 3 - May 12, 2010 – 7PM

Werner set up samples for viewing under the recently procured Ultra Fast Electron Microscope which was capable of taking 4-D movies of molecules. The microscope was a modified transmission electron microscope interfaced with an ultra fast laser. It was capable of capturing 3-dimensional structural changes of molecules over very short time spans. He first looked at the samples under low power, about 10X. He then increased the magnification in increments of 50X up to 500X, taking photo-scans at each power setting.

Each of the straight-from-the-leak samples (no OxiMax mixed in) looked fairly normal except for a faint gray-like crystalline molecule suspended within adjacent hydrocarbon molecules. This alien molecule didn't appear to be bonded chemically to the hydrocarbons. At first Werner thought it might be only an artifact of something that really wasn't there. But each sample had some of these "parasite like" molecules. They did appear slightly larger in the samples of crude closer to the surface and in the samples that had been mixed in the crude oil plume, suggesting that time of exposure to sea water and/or sunlight might be a factor. They weren't different enough to justify retests, so he proceeded to the samples mixed with the OxiMax #7.

In comparison to the non-mixed specimens, the mixed samples

did show some degradation of the longer chained hydrocarbons, which was the desired result. But the parasite molecules still remained.

Werner then decided to deviate from the test protocol. Because of his vast experience, he usually was given permission to modify test procedures without getting approvals from higher ups. He wanted to determine if more vigorous mixing would alter the results. He rationalized that this might occur if severe weather, like a hurricane, would move into the area after the OxiMax had been sprayed onto the oil plume.

Werner chose two samples of the medium concentration of OxiMax in the crude oil from the surface. He put these samples through a combination of centrifuge, then high-level shaker. As he placed the sample under the microscope at 300X, he saw something so shocking he poked his eye into the microscope lens, knocking the microscope out of focus. At first he thought he must have blinked at the wrong time. As he refocused the microscope, it happened again. The gray parasite molecule appeared to consume the wall of the adjacent hydrocarbon molecule. It was as if it were alive. "Holy shit!" he yelled and almost fell backwards off the bench he was sitting on.

He reached for the second sample test tube to see if it was reacting the same way. He was trembling with so much excitement that he spilled some of the solution on his arm. The mixture was slimy and slid down the sleeve of his lab coat and contacted the skin on the back of his hand. It felt surprisingly warm to the touch. There was still some of the second sample left, so he brushed the spill off his hand and feverishly worked to prepare another specimen from the remaining second sample, which took about 10 minutes. It only partially registered in his mind that all of a sudden his hand felt cool.

He placed the second sample under the microscope and immediately recognized that the gray molecule was now nearly

100 times larger than any he had seen before. It also seemed to be pulsating. About 30 minutes had elapsed since he spilled the mixture onto his hand. It was now that it registered in his mind that he felt a tingling sensation in his arm.

Werner rushed over to the sink and flushed his hand and arm with tap water. The sensation quickly changed from tingling to a dull ache. But worse, he now felt a crushing sensation in his lungs. Werner was keenly aware of what a heart attack felt like, and this wasn't the same.

In the back of his mind a message flashed that he better call for help. As he tried to move toward the phone, he suddenly realized he had trouble moving in any direction let alone in a straight line toward the phone. He staggered in what seemed to be a random pattern as his mind was losing the ability to concentrate. His chest now felt like it was being crushed in a vise, and he abruptly fell to the floor. His eyes were open and the lab seemed to be rotating around him. As the pain in his chest intensified to an unbearable level, darkness slowly overcame him. The last thing he felt between the waves of pain was a warm fluid flowing through the veins in his neck.

Chapter 4 - May12, 2010 – 10:45 PM

T im had definitely scored with Tina. After pizza, Tim and Tina went to his place. It had been a wild night and he lost track of time. It was 10:45 when he realized he better do something fast. He dialed up the lab but got no answer. He looked at Tina, who seemed sound asleep. He gave her arm a shake and she groggily looked up at him.

"Tina, I've got to go back to the lab before my shift is over. Do me a favor and don't mention our date. I could get into a lot of trouble at work." He also realized that there could be consequences because he now knew her true age was 16.

"Don't worry. If my Dad finds out where I've been and that I went out with a much older guy, I'll be grounded for a year."

"Ok look," said Tim. "I'll drop you off by your girlfriend's house and you can figure out an alibi with her. Then call home to ask if you can stay the night at her house."

"Tim, you're so smart," giggled Tina.

Tim dropped her off and was back to the lab by 11:00 PM. He thought he had really pushed the envelope this time. After entering the lab thru the back door, he looked around and didn't see anyone. At first he hoped Gramps had bugged out early, but deep down he knew better. He picked up the phone to the decontamination lab and let it ring at least six times. There was no answer. He walked over to the thick glass viewing window and peered in. At first he saw nothing, but then saw a pool of red liquid that looked like it might be blood coming from behind the side of the microscope base. It was such a huge machine he really couldn't see around it, but then he noticed a reflection from a piece of polished Plexiglas they used to make specimen racks. Tim suddenly felt sick. He managed to call the plant 911 number before losing his partially digested pizza in the lab sink.

Tim gathered himself enough to think up a story to tell the manager. He thought to himself that Tim Gardner could still come out looking like a hero.

Chapter 5 - May 13, 2010 – 8AM

Jimmy Sterling strode anxiously toward the recently converted DC3 crop duster. His co-pilot, Tony Duprea, was already in the cockpit running through the checklist. Tony jokingly yelled, "Hey Sterling, how many more trips do you think this crate can make?"

"It won't make one more if you screw up that checklist," he replied.

The DC3 was a World War 2 vintage twin piston engine plane that was still flying with some third world countries and low cost contractors, that is, if you could find parts for the plane. It could fly low and slow, which was great for crop dusting or other cargo drops if needed. This one was pressed into service under contract from GG Oil to spray dispersal agents onto the crude oil belching into the Gulf of Mexico from the deep water oil leak. Sterling had used it as a crop duster up until the Deep Water Horizon oil platform blew up and sank nearly a month ago.

"We better get moving pronto!" Sterling announced. "The weather report predicts some violent thunderstorms around the leak site in about three hours with the possibility of waterspouts. We've got a new oil dispersal chemical called OxiMax #7 the boss wants to try out. It's supposed to react with the salt water, generate oxygen, and oxidize the crude oil. That'll help eliminate the crude oil before it gets close to land."

Tony quipped, "Sure that's what those genius GG Oil geeks say. I think one of those guys was in my high school chemistry class. He recommended an experiment that blew up and damn near burnt the school down."

"Ok, ok let's get serious. We're gassed up and the chemical tanks are full."

Moments later they got clearance from the tower and were underway. The DC3 was nicknamed "The Gunny Bird," and rightfully so. It took about 45 minutes to get to the main oil plume called the "Larson Slick" which became clearly visible in the water. It appeared as an ugly brown surface scar as they approached from the Southeast.

"God, what a fricking mess," Tony commented. "If I had GG stock, I'd sell it ASAP. This is going to cost them big time."

"Yeah," Sterling replied, "and they should pay every penny plus fines for shortcutting the safety measures. This never should have happened. Ok, we're supposed to dump this shit right into the middle of the plume. Let's fly past it then turn around and fly from west to east and dump our load. I don't like the size of those cumulus clouds building to the west."

They made their pass, dumped the load of chemicals, and then headed for home.

"All we need are a couple of waterspouts to stir things up and maybe the resulting mutant fish will only have three eyes on one head instead of three heads with three eyes each," joked Tony.

"Careful what you wish for," noted Sterling with a troubled look. "Reality has a knack of coming back and biting us in the butt."

Chapter 6 - June 1, 2010 – 8:00 AM

B eauregard Calhoun, or Beau as he liked to be called, sat on his front porch swinging slowly on his giant glider. His home, a true southern-style plantation home, was a testament to his life and social status in the elite circles of Baton Rouge, Louisiana.

Beau claimed to be a "good ole boy" but had a drive and ruthlessness second to none. He had built an empire of sorts consisting of home developments, condominiums, and four-star hotels stretching from the Louisiana coast through the panhandle of Florida. He, however, was never satisfied, and as he neared his 65th birthday, he wanted most to build a Southern Plantation Resort that would make Louisiana a year-round tourist destination rivaling Orlando, Florida. Before he died, he also wanted to place the name Beauregard Calhoun right up there with Jean Baptiste Lemoyne & Edward Douglass White in the Louisiana history books.

For over 25 years Beau had designed this plantation resort in his mind. Twenty years ago he had selected a stretch of coastal Louisiana several hundred miles west of New Orleans. He had even begun the long permitting process. Unfortunately for Beau, a deal made in Washington, DC designated the land as a wildlife preserve, which stymied his plans.

Beau was never one to surrender and considered the set-back as only a lost battle. The war had just started. He decided on a different route to get what he wanted. He learned over the years you couldn't win in the political game unless you became part of it, so he became a player in the local, then state, and ultimately the national political machine. Although Louisiana by itself did not have a significant number of electoral votes, in the last three national elections Beau was instrumental in aligning the southern states of Mississippi, Alabama, and Louisiana into a significant voting block. Plus, he was the leading supporter and close friend of Louisiana Senator Clarence R. Lee.

As Beau rocked slowly in the humid summer night air, a smile creased its way across his face. This might just be the time to call in some chips. Beau was adept at finding a favorable spin in any disaster. Right now was the mother of all disasters, especially for his area of the country.

Nightly news on all the networks was covering the massive crude oil leak spewing from the deep water well in the Gulf of Mexico. Numerous attempts to stop the deep earth hemorrhaging had failed. The huge oil slick's impact to the environment was unimaginable and getting worse by the hour. Yet Beau had a different perspective. This just might be the chance to remove his chosen property from the protected status. What the hell, the pristine coastal marshes and swamps were going to be ruined anyway along with much of the wildlife. And just in case, by some freak of luck, the oil missed "his" land, Beau had a plan B.

Chapter 7 - June 1, 2010 – 8:30 AM

L ike Beauregard Calhoun, Quinton Jones rocked on his porch also. It was there that the similarities ended. Contrary to Beau Calhoun, Quinton Jones was on the other side of the economic ladder. He lived in a modest home near the bayous he fished for a living. Quinn, as his friends called him, was from Bayou Cane, a small fishing village on the Louisiana coast. His dad had a fishing boat, and fishing had been a part of his family for generations. His financial position was not for the want of smarts. In fact, he had had a bright future in college, both academically and athletically.

In high school Quinn had lettered in football as a wide receiver and was actively recruited at numerous colleges. Unfortunately, a knee injury in a final all star high school game ended a promising career. The athletic scholarship offers ended with that game and with it the opportunity for big name colleges. The family fishing business paid the bills, but little was left for college away from home. So Quinn ended up going to a local junior college. That was 20 years ago.

It was in junior college that Quinn was introduced to what soon became his second passion next to fishing, and that was archeology. He won numerous honors for papers he wrote on the Pre-Cambrian and Cambrian eras of the earth's archeological history. To this day, he'd take local high school and junior college students on fossil hunting trips.

While in junior college, Quinn met the love he thought he'd live his life with, LeAnn Roberts. But again, fate entered his life when his father had a deadly heart attack. With no money coming in and he being an only child, Quinn had to drop out of college to run his Dad's fishing boat.

Quinn worked hard, but now his livelihood was threatened by the very ocean he loved. Actually the ocean was only the messenger. The currents that brought life up the food chain were now bringing the dreaded man-made tide of crude oil that threatened all life in its path.

Quinn lay on a hammock fastened precariously between two knotty Cypress trees. Fishing had been banned a week ago from his favorite spots since crude oil tar balls were spotted floating in the area. But to Quinn, an even bigger concern was the layer of crude oil reportedly moving several feet below the water's surface. Supposedly the droplets of oil resulted from chemical dispersants airdropped onto the crude oil plume. This layer could filter out sunlight and also kill the plankton that the smaller bait fish feed on if it didn't kill the bait fish outright. With the bait fish gone, the larger game fish would soon follow.

About a week after the explosion that created the oil leak, Quinn and some of the other fisherman went out to the leak site. There were numerous oil company and government ships taking samples of the crude as it reached the surface. Initially, Quinn thought this was probably routine as part of the failure investigation. Yesterday he returned to the spill site. The site was a beehive of activity with converted fishing boats donning skimmers to try to capture the crude, as well as oil company vessels working various schemes to try to cap or at least reduce the size of the leak. Quinn kept a safe upwind distance, partially because of the smell that had forced many to return after only hours at the site, but he also wanted to avoid interfering with any of the ongoing capping efforts.

After being there for less than 10 minutes, Quinn was hailed by a ship flying a Homeland Security flag below the stars and stripes. He was boarded, asked for identification and then, without any pleasantries, asked to leave immediately. The officer implied it was for Quinn's own safety, but there seemed to be an unmistakably confrontational tone in the officer's manner. Initially, Quinn figured nerves were frayed all around and chalked it up to long hours with no end in sight. But as he turned his boat toward home, the sun caught the darkened windows of the bridge of the Homeland Security vessel just right, revealing what looked like full HAZMAT suits on those running the ship. There was something wrong with that picture.

As he swayed in his hammock, Quinn ran an instant replay in his mind over and over with no refutable evidence to overrule his concerns. Just then, he was startled by the annoying ring tone he meant to change on his cell phone. That call changed his life forever, and would soon prove that things he thought were most important, would be trivial in comparison.

Chapter 8 - June 1, 2010 – 9:00 AM

The call was from Quinn's best friend, Jesse Carter. They had been close since high school where they met during football tryouts. Jesse played linebacker and was an imposing figure at 6'3, 240 lbs of lean muscle. Jesse had a reputation of taking out wide receivers on quick in patterns, and Quinn was sure glad they were on the same team. Jesse joined the marines after high school and had been on several missions that he claimed he couldn't talk about. One thing was for sure, Jesse was a guy you wanted on your side if trouble broke out.

Jesse put in 20 years in the Marines, then retired and was doing odd construction jobs until something more permanent came along. Jesse had married Ginger Sloan shortly after joining the Marines. Quinn had been the best man and thought the world of Ginger. Ginger was a nurse on base at the time and had since become an RN. She was now head nurse at the only major hospital in the area, so she was presently the bread winner of their family, which also consisted of three children, Samantha, Kyle, and Devon.

Quinn could tell by Jesse's voice on the phone that he was riled up. Quinn knew you didn't want Jesse riled. "Calm down, Jesse. What the hell is going on?"

Jesse nearly yelled, "Did you hear the latest news from the spill site? They brought in at least four body bags last night."

"Jesus!" gasped Quinn. "Who were they?"

"Don't know yet, but Ginger is trying to find out what happened. Why don't you come over about 5:00 for dinner tonight. It's been awhile and the kids always look forward to your fish stories. Maybe we'll have some updates."

"I'll be there."

But the more Quinn thought about it, the more he didn't want to wait until tonight to find out what was going on. Ever since being run off by the Homeland Security boat, Quinn had a bad feeling about the entire situation. The deaths could have simply been an accident unrelated to the spill or…. The answer just festered in his mind.

He decided to call Ginger at the hospital. After standing by while she was paged, Ginger finally came on the line. "Hi Ginger," Quinn said urgently. "I spoke briefly with Jesse and he said there were some bodies that had come in from the leak site. What do you know about the situation?"

Ginger whispered into the phone, "Something really strange is going on. The medical examiner requested an autopsy even before the bodies arrived, so someone high up was already notified there was a problem. As you know, the medical examiner's office and labs are in the basement of our hospital. The bodies arrived around 2AM. According to the in-coming log, at 2:15 AM a Division of Homeland Security van arrived with six officers. They claimed this was a national security issue and therefore had jurisdiction. The local police and medical examiner got into a shouting match with Homeland Security. Right now everything is at a standstill, except the bodies were sealed and stored in special handling isolation vaults."

Just then Quinn heard strained voices in the background and Ginger said she had to get off and would try to call back later. "Homeland Security again," he said to himself. "Why are they involved at all? No one has suggested the Deep Water Horizon explosion was terrorist related. Of course we're not always told the truth either."

Quinn made up his mind right then he was going to get to the bottom of this. After all, this was his home, and his livelihood was at stake. He decided to take a drastic step. He never had much use for the news media, but in this case for a change they might actually do what they were supposed to. In his mind that was to investigate a story until they found out the truth, and then inform the public in a factual manner.

He decided to call a local newspaper reporter named Grace Connelly. She had done an article on him last year, mainly because her oldest son was part of a group he took on a fossil hunt. It was really only a filler article that made the middle of the local section of the paper, but she had done good research and said she'd return the favor if he needed something in the future. That's exactly what he needed right now.

It was nearing lunch time and Quinn wanted to act fast. He decided he'd suggest to Grace that he had a story that might interest her and ask if they could discuss it over lunch. He dialed her office, got transferred to her extension, and to his surprise she picked up on the first ring. After exchanging pleasantries, Quinn tried to be convincing without revealing what his real motive was. Grace didn't show much interest and seemed perturbed at how vague Quinn was. She finally gave him what Quinn thought was the brush-off, using an excuse of must attend meetings and appointments starting at lunchtime until late afternoon. Quinn even reminded her of her offer of returning the interview favor he'd given her. Finally, sensing his disappointment and not wanting to renege on an offer, Grace said she could meet for lunch tomorrow at 11:30.

This was not what Quinn had hoped for and he felt frustrated. He flipped on the TV to catch the lunch time local news. A news flash grabbed his attention like a bolt of lightening, "Huge fish kill reported in the Gulf of Mexico in the vicinity of the largest of the oil slicks." Aerial photos had determined the oil slicks had broken into several smaller ones and winds and currents were moving them in different directions. The largest, called the "Larson Slick" was getting dangerously close to the Louisiana coast.

Quinn had expected damage to fish, but nothing this fast. The fish being described were not only bait fish but also larger game fish. There were reports of some species of shark and some dolphin dying, although these reports were supposedly not confirmed. Quinn started pacing back and forth. He wanted to do something but didn't know what. He decided to gather some small coolers and plastic bags and go down to the beach. He figured he just might get some samples of any sea life that might wash up, although he had no idea what he'd do with them.

The beach was only about a 15-minute drive. It was a typical hot, muggy, and hazy Gulf Coast day. After parking, he decided to leave the coolers in the truck. He walked onto the beach down one of the pedestrian access paths and was surprised at how few people were around. Other than that, everything seemed normal, except it was dead calm with not a breath of breeze. He had brought a towel with him and lay down near the water's edge. With closed eyes, he listened to the gentle waves washing ashore. He could hear the rumble of a thunderstorm off in the distance. As he drifted off to sleep, he imagined that this was like the proverbial calm before the storm.

Chapter 9 - June 1, 2010 – 4PM

S uddenly Quinn was inside some Plexiglas pipe squeezing tightly against his shoulder. He could see someone outside but they couldn't hear him yelling at them. Quinn jolted to consciousness with a bright light shining in his face. A policeman was pushing on his shoulder, directing a beam of light from his flashlight into Quinn's eyes, and yelling, "Hey buddy, are you all right?"

Quinn, his throat scratchy dry, replied, "Whoa! I really must have dozed off." It wasn't dark, but a thunderstorm had closed in, blotting out the sun.

The cop said jokingly, "With all the talk of things dying at sea, I thought maybe you washed up as well. You're Quinton Jones, aren't you? You took me and my father out fishing last year. We caught a couple of nice sailfish. My dad still talks about that day."

"Yes, I'm Quinn, and now I recognize you. Hector Lopez, right?"

"Yep."

"I came down here to see if there were any fish washing up. Fish kills are almost like dollar bills floating out of my wallet. Hector, what do you hear about the fish kill?"

Hector squinted his eyes. "I hear it's pretty bad. I expect the beach will be closed tomorrow, so you better enjoy it while you can."

Quinn wanted to pump Hector for more information, so he continued, "Hey Hector. I heard rumors there were some guys that died near the spill site. Do you know anything about that?"

Hector's disposition suddenly turned cool. "No," he answered curtly. "I've got a lot of beach to patrol, so I better get moving. I recommend you stay away from the beach until the health department gives the all clear. Check the news or radio stations for the current update. See you later." With that, Hector hurried off almost like telling lies was not his nature.

Quinn shook his head, hoping that might bring clarity to all the questions spinning in his mind. It didn't help. He glanced at his watch and realized he must have slept for a couple of hours. He had a sinking feeling that he was lucky he got some sleep in now because life might soon be switching to overdrive.

He hustled from the beach to get a shower before heading over to Jesse's for dinner. Quinn muttered to himself, "I haven't accomplished a damn thing since this morning."

Chapter 10 - June 1, 2010 – 5:15 PM

Q uinn grabbed a couple of six packs and arrived at Jesse's a little after 5:00 PM. He rang the doorbell, and the door flew open. He was met by a chorus of three high-pitched voices all talking at once. Jesse's kids were so happy and full of life. They all had questions about the oil spill and where oil came from and how it was formed. Ginger joined trying to calm down the excitement. Ginger laughingly said, "Ok kids, at least let Professor Jones get in the door. I'm still finishing up the salad and Jesse's still grilling the roast so you have a few minutes to conduct class."

Quinn knew he'd never get to eat unless he at least tried to answer. Actually, the kids' questions were good medicine as it took his mind off the real problem, at least for now.

Devon was the youngest, but was really sharp. He wanted to know how oil was formed. Quinn knew Devon read a lot, so he wanted to keep his expert status, at least in the kids' eyes, but not talk over his head either. He started to explain, "Most geologists believe oil comes from decaying plants and animals, mostly small sea life, like plankton and algae. But plants and animals can get into the mix in swamps and riverbeds. This dead life falls to the sea floor or riverbed or swamp bottom. With time they get buried under layers of sediment which builds pressure and temperature, converting the material into a waxy-like material called kerogen that eventually breaks down into crude oil."

Kyle piped up, "What if the plants or animals were sick? Would the oil end up with their diseases?"

For a brief instant something flashed in Quinn's mind, but it was gone just as fast. "Well, probably not. The bacteria or virus would probably be destroyed by all the heat and pressure."

Samantha, the oldest, asked, "You said most geologists believe this. Is there another theory?"

"Well, yes. There is a theory that chemical reactions deep within the earth combine existing carbon, again at high temperature and pressure, into hydrocarbons which after a long period of time become oil. There is even a third theory that suggests that oil is the byproduct of the life cycle of deep earth dwelling microbes." Again a shadow of a thought crossed deep in the back of Quinn's mind, but was gone as fast as a shadow from a cloud.

Just then, the appetizing smell of a perfectly cooked roast teased all of their nostrils as Jesse came in from the back porch. "There seems to be a lot of profound thinking going on in here," laughed Jesse. "How about some good old-fashioned southern cooking?"

They had a truly enjoyable dinner, but all the adults could sense tension trying not to discuss the day's events until after the kids left the table.

Finally, with the table cleared and the kids going outside to play badminton, they got down to business. Quinn could no longer contain himself. "Ginger, what happened at the hospital? You never called me back."

Ginger was really getting angry, which was unusual for her. "They put a blackout on all outside calls."

"Who did?" barked Jesse.

"All managers and supervisors got on a conference call with James Simmons, the regional director of Homeland Security. He said it was vital to national security and that no information was to leave the hospital."

Jesse almost knocked over his chair. "This is bull. Something's rotten here."

Quinn was about to say something when Ginger held up her hand. "There's more," she said. "We never got to do an autopsy. In fact, no one at the hospital even saw the bodies. At about 2:30, an unmarked refrigerated truck arrived and Homeland Security agents escorted the sealed body vaults into the truck. Apparently, there was a private discussion between that James Simmons, our police chief, the chairman of the hospital board of directors, and rumor is that US Senator Lee was also on the call. The truck left about an hour later. No paperwork, no nothing."

Jesse and Quinn looked dumbfounded at one another. Quinn finally said, "Why would a US Senator and a Homeland Security director be involved in this? This has gotten up the food chain awfully fast. You know we'll never know the truth unless we find it out ourselves."

Ginger and Jesse nodded solemnly.

"But we need a plan. Any ideas?"

Ginger glumly stated, "I know I'll get stonewalled at the hospital. Besides, except for the chairman of the board, I don't think anyone else knows much. I'm at a loss on where to turn."

"I'm clueless," said Jesse. "If there was somebody's ass to whoop, I'd be right on it. But this... We need someone like a private investigator."

"Hey, wait a minute, that might be a place to start," Quinn said anxiously. "Jesse, do you have any ex-marine buddies you could contact? Maybe one of them or someone they know could do some investigative work. It would have to be someone we can trust."

"I'll work on that," replied Jesse with a glimmer of hope in his voice.

Quinn thought a moment then suggested, "I guess you heard about the fish kill. I went to the beach to have a look, but nothing had washed in yet. I think I'll get up before dawn and go down there again. I thought I'd get some samples of the fish if there are any. I hadn't figured out what I'd do with them, but it seemed like they might come in handy, perhaps as evidence."

"You'd better get there before that friggen Homeland Security truck does!" hissed Jesse.

"Be careful Quinn," Ginger jumped in. "Be sure to wear rubber gloves and a surgical mask. We don't know what we're dealing with. I'll get you some right now. I always carry them in a kit in the car." She hurried off to the garage.

Jesse looked at Quinn and asked, "Quinn, what about your old girlfriend LeAnn?"

"What about her?" stammered Quinn. "Where did that come from anyway? I got over her years ago."

"I didn't mean it like that," laughed Jesse. "I was just thinking about the fish specimens. Isn't she a renowned biologist and veterinarian? Maybe you could get her to do the analysis."

"Damn, you're right!" grinned Quinn. "Jesse, I knew you were good for something. That thought deserves a beer."

Just then Ginger returned with some gloves and masks. Quinn passed out three tall ones. Clinking their beer bottles together Quinn toasted, "For better or worse," not knowing it was going to get worse... much, much worse.

Chapter 11 - June 2, 2010 – 4AM

After a couple more beers, Quinn left Jesse's and headed home. After talking it over with Jesse and Ginger, he decided he'd call LeAnn sometime tomorrow morning. Jesse wanted to go with Quinn to the beach in the morning, but Quinn wanted Jesse to focus on finding a private eye.

After showering, Quinn laid in bed for hours thinking about what to do next. He tossed and turned all night, not really sleeping much. He was used to getting up early to prepare his boat for a day of fishing, at least before the oil leak burst on the scene. So he finally dragged out of bed at 4AM. He went to the kitchen, got two small coolers and filled them with ice. He changed his mind though and removed some of the ice from one cooler, put a couple of beers in, then added back some more ice. He figured he'd use this as a decoy in case the cops or homeland security agents stopped him and wanted to see what was inside. He thought to himself that he was getting paranoid, but he really felt he needed some actual sea life samples to help find out what was happening. He also sensed there were others who didn't want anyone to know the real story.

Trying to think clearly this early without much sleep was a challenge. For the second cooler Quinn wanted some insurance in case it was checked. He rubbed his stubble of a beard for a moment. Thinking out loud he said, "What I need is a false bottom."

Looking up, he spotted the old fashioned drop ceiling mottled plastic that covered his kitchen fluorescent lights. The stuff was thin and made in 12 inch x 12 inch squares. It was kind of yellowed with age and just might pass as a bottom, especially before dawn. He dragged down a section, then cut a piece out of it that fit fairly well in the bottom of the cooler. He then took it out, put a layer of ice in the bottom of the cooler, slid in the false bottom, then put the rest of the ice in a zip lock bag, and put this bag on top.

Feeling pretty proud of himself, he closed up the coolers, put on some old shorts and a tee shirt, and was ready to head for the beach. He started out the door, but decided he'd better take some spare zip-lock bags to put the samples in. He grabbed those and started out again, but stopped by the door thinking he was missing something. His mind was spinning but coming up empty.

He opened the door to his pickup when it hit him. "I better take the rubber gloves and surgical masks Ginger gave me," he said out loud. He'd put them by his nightstand the night before. He raced up the steps grabbed them and headed for the door a third time. He stopped cold. Thinking out loud again he said, "If I show up at the beach with gloves and a mask, I'll look way too obvious." He was wide awake now. He rushed back upstairs. Rummaging through his closet he found what he was looking for. He had an old raggedy fanny pack he used to carry all sorts of things when he fished with his dad. It was big enough to carry the masks and gloves and didn't look out of place. "Yeah, perfect," he said. He put the coolers in the cab instead of the truck bed just to make sure they didn't bounce or blow out the back.

Chapter 12 - June 2, 2010 – 5:15AM

Quinn arrived at the beach at about 5:15AM. Dawn hadn't cracked the sky yet. As he opened the truck door, the smell hit him square in the nose. It was the smell of death. Although he didn't see anyone, he was hesitant on donning the surgical mask just yet. He didn't want to look like he was on a scavenging mission.

He grabbed the coolers, took a last deep breath of air from the truck cab, and headed toward the water. What he saw nearly knocked the breath right out of him. The tide was going out and the beach was littered with dead fish of all sizes. There were dead crabs, lobsters, and clams in amongst the carnage. He almost stepped on a rotting raccoon a few yards from the line of death. To his surprise the creatures were not all coated with oil like the pelican and other sea bird pictures the TV news casts kept repeating over and over. This sea life looked fairly normal, at least at first glance.

His eyes panned down the beach, and although it was still dark, it looked like this scene was repeated as far as he could see. He looked up and down the beach and thought he saw some figures moving about a quarter mile away. But distances were deceiving and he couldn't tell whether they were walking or picking things up. One thing he knew for sure, they weren't surf casting.

Quinn felt he better get samples and get the hell out before the bad guys, whoever they were, showed up. As he bent over to put down the coolers, the stench almost overpowered him. He was used to fish aromas, but this was much worse. He slipped the surgical mask and gloves out of his pouch fumbling with them before finally getting them on. He cursed himself for not practicing putting them on the night before. It cost him precious minutes. He lifted the bag of ice and false bottom out of the second cooler and grabbed a plastic bag out of his pocket.

He looked around trying to decide which might be the best sample. He realized he should have spoken with LeAnn first. Suddenly he wasn't feeling so proud of himself.

He decided he'd get a few of each type of sea creature. Some of the fish had hunks bitten out of them, probably from crabs or other fish. So he picked a fish about 12 inches long that looked pretty much intact. But as he picked it up, Quinn couldn't believe how light it was. It was as if some thing sucked the insides out of it. The fish's skin almost collapsed around his hand. He slipped the carcass into a plastic bag. He got a couple of smaller fish, a lobster, some crabs, and some clams, putting each type of sea life into a separate plastic bag. He also saw a jellyfish that looked almost black rather then their normal clear coloration. He chose not to include that because he already had enough to fill the cooler.

He placed each bag carefully into the cooler, slid the false bottom in place, then dumped the ice out of the plastic bag to cover things up. By now the eastern sky showed the first signs that dawn was approaching. Quinn took off his mask and gloves and stuffed them back into his fanny pack. With a little more light he noticed there was an unusually large amount of seaweed and some sea grass along the water line. This was adding to the foul odor. But the seaweed didn't look normal. The stems were almost a reddish brown color with black edges. Using the ice bag he just emptied, he picked up a small bunch and started stuffing it into the last plastic bag he had. Just then a deep, almost growling voice behind him yelled, "Hey, what the hell do you think you're doing?"

Quinn spun around, nearly jumping out of his sneakers, and dropped the plastic bag of seaweed in the process. He was face to face with a square-jawed, shaved head man about 6 feet tall wearing a Homeland Security windbreaker and sunglasses. The guy looked plain mean, and without a hint of a smile asked again, "What are you doing with that seaweed?"

The guy was definitely not from the South, but Quinn couldn't place where he'd heard the accent before. Quinn's throat suddenly felt like dry toast. Trying to think fast, he managed to rasp out, "I was going to fix some fish in a smoker and usually wrap it in seaweed."

"That so?" said the guy. "You wouldn't be trying to bull shit me, would ya? Let me see what's in the coolers."

"You got a warrant?" snapped Quinn.

"I don't need one, and I can arrest you on the spot if I choose. You see what this says on my jacket, or maybe I shouldn't assume you can read," the guy sneered.

Quinn could feel the hairs on the back of his neck rising up and knew this might come to blows shortly. "Look" Quinn said. "I could buy a jacket like that at Kmart. How do I know you're not some fagot trying to grab my stuff?"

Quinn could see the guy's neck muscles stiffening up. Quinn continued, "I have a right to see an ID, don't I? Or maybe I shouldn't assume you are a citizen of this country." Quinn saw the guy starting to ball his hands into fists, but by now was too pissed to care. He could hold his own in a fight, but saw out of the corner of his eye another guy with a similar jacket hustling toward them.

"Hey Harbaugh, is there a problem here?" yelled the second guy. This guy's accent was definitely Southern, which helped Quinn relax a little.

"Yeah," said Harbaugh. "This smart ass refused to show me what's in his coolers."

"I didn't refuse, I just wanted to see some ID first," countered Quinn, who was starting to get himself under control.

The second guy flashed his ID. His name was Clemmons. "We're who we say we are." announced Clemmons.

"Well, your friend Hardsmell didn't say who he was," said Quinn.

"The name's Harbaugh," growled Harbaugh. With that, Harbaugh grabbed Quinn's cooler closest to him, turned it upside down, and dumped the contents onto the sand. Unfortunately it was the second cooler. The ice, false bottom, and plastic bags with the specimens hit the sand with a thud. Quinn realized right then he should have thought this through and added something to hold the false bottom in. He clenched his teeth and cursed to himself.

"Well, well. Looks like you were planning a real clambake. Got some fish, some crabs, some clams all neatly packaged," mocked Harbaugh. "You really are an idiot. Can't you read the signs saying the beach is closed because of contamination? Oh, wait, I forgot you're reading impaired. Let's cuff him. If he falls a couple times on the way back to the cruiser and gets sand in his eyes, that would be a shame, wouldn't it."

Just then a 3rd man walked up. It was Hector Lopez. Quinn, trying to defend himself said, "There were no signs up when I got here. Last I heard you could get fish with the proper license and I have a commercial license."

Hector added, "Give the guy a break. He has been here awhile because I checked his truck and the motor was cool. He is a commercial fisherman and an ok guy."

Quinn thought to himself, "Why were they checking my truck in the first place?" Harbaugh just scowled.

Then Harbaugh realized he hadn't checked the other cooler. He turned it upside down, spilling the ice and beer cans, which clanked together on a pile of seaweed. "Hey Clemmons, you want a cool one?" sneered Harbaugh.

Clemmons just shook his head no. With that Harbaugh stomped on each can, emptying the contents onto the seaweed and sand.

"There you go, dipshit," Harbaugh said with a victorious smile. "Beer soaked seaweed should really add some flavor to your grillin."

Clemmons finally said, "I think we're done here. Mr. Jones we're going to let you go, but leave the beach immediately. If we catch you here again, we'll arrest you for loitering and obstruction of justice."

Harbaugh looked disappointed. Quinn asked if he could get his coolers. Harbaugh saw the chance for a last jibe. "You can have the coolers, but we'll keep the packaged goodies. You could make a seaweed sandwich though." With that he kicked some sand and seaweed into the first cooler which was lying on its side. Quinn knew going to jail wouldn't help their cause, so he just bent over and picked up both coolers.

As he started to leave, Quinn turned to the trio and stated, "I thought you Homeland Security guys were supposed to be patriots, not pussies like Hardsmell here."

Harbaugh started to move toward Quinn, but Clemmons held his arm.

"Something's rotten with this whole picture, and it seems like you guys are helping the wrong side," Quinn added. With that he turned and left. As he trudged toward his truck, he noticed there were now teams of Homeland Security men combing the beach using front end loaders to pick up all the dead sea life.

Chapter 13 - June 2, 2010 – 7:00 AM

As he walked toward his truck, Quinn felt emotionally drained. He'd been totally defeated and humiliated at the same time. He had no samples and now virtually no chance of getting any. His only positive thought was that it was a good thing that Jesse hadn't come with him. Both of them would probably be in jail while an evacuation team tried to pull the heads of Harbaugh and Clemmons out of the sand. Quinn almost smiled at that thought.

As he got into his truck, his mind sparked like spinning a lighter flint. There were some private houses on the beach about three miles from the public beach. Some were new, but there was one old home that had been there since before he was born. A Cajun family named Trudeau had lived there for over 50 years. The home was very old and now rundown since only the mother in her late eighties was still living. Her husband used to crew for Quinn's dad, but had passed away most likely from continual heavy drinking. Quinn's dad used to bring the family fresh fish once a week, and Quinn continued the practice until the oil leak put a stop to his fishing.

Quinn knew he would be taking a chance, but thought maybe he could talk Mrs. Trudeau into sneaking out to the beach and getting some samples either later this morning or tonight. He didn't know how long fish would be washing in. He didn't want to wait too long since he thought decomposed fish might not provide a good specimen.

Quinn made a quick left from the main beach road and headed west. He kept checking his rear view mirror to be sure he wasn't followed. He was totally paranoid now. He turned onto RUE James Street and pulled into a mostly sand driveway that lead several hundred yards through a live oak canopy before arriving at the house. The home was a small clapboard bungalow and weeds had pretty much overgrown the front yard. At night the place was downright creepy.

As he approached the front door, he noticed the front window was open halfway. He heard an old woman weeping somewhere in the back of the house. He called out, "Mrs. Trudeau, it's Quinton Jones." For some reason she always called him Quinton instead of Quinn. He yelled a little louder, "Are you all right?" The sobbing continued so he hurried around the side of the house and opened the gate that led to the back yard.

"Mrs. Trudeau it's Quinton. Are you all right?" he called again. This time she must have heard him because for a moment there was silence.

As he got to the back of the house, he spotted her leaning up against a shovel. She appeared to be digging a small grave and a large Tupperware cake saver like container sat next to the grave. Quinn couldn't tell what was inside.

"Mrs. Trudeau what happened?" asked Quinn as he reached out to comfort her. He could see the tears smearing down her wrinkled, saddened face. Her gray hair was all tangled with sweat and dirt.

"Oh, Quinton it's you. I thought maybe those rude, emotionless bastards were back again."

"You mean the Homeland Security people?" Quinn couldn't believe they'd already covered this part of the beach. Then he spotted the yellow crime scene tape hung between hedges covering the path from her backyard to the beach. It said "No Entry Violators Will Be Prosecuted" in bold black letters.

"Yeah, that was them. They're the ones that should be prosecuted. My home has right of way all the way to the water. It was deeded to us from the State back when a person really had some rights. Now they're telling me I can't go onto the beach until they give the all clear. Who do they think they're dealing with? Ronny would have sent them packing with a load of buckshot in their ass." Ronny was her deceased husband, and from the stories Quinn's dad told, Ronny would have done just that.

"I'm so sorry, Mrs. Trudeau. I had a run in with them this morning myself. But what are you doing digging out here in the heat?" The fire in her eyes faded just as fast as it sprang up.

"Chrissy, my cat, was the last thing left in the world that I loved. This morning about 4AM I heard her meowing in a pitiful, fearful way. She must have been down at the beach. She'd go there sometimes at night to chase crabs. She was trying to crawl back through the hedges and was calling for me to help her. I was cooking us some breakfast of black beans and rice since neither one of us sleeps good at night anymore. I still had my cooking mittens on and I ran out to help her." The tears started streaming down her face again. She struggled with words as her voiced cracked, "I was too late. Yesterday she was fine and playful. She sat in my lap purring while we watched the late night news. Now she's gone. I keep asking GOD why... why my Chrissy? I can't imagine being without her. She was my buddy... my constant companion."

She took a deep breath, then spoke like the tough lady she was. "I placed Chrissy in that cake tin yonder and was starting to bury her when those jokers showed up. I slid her under the porch before they came in the back. They wanted to know what I was doing, like they had any right to know. I told them I was digging a hole and was going to put some dead fish in for fertilizer like the Indians used to do. They got a chuckle out of that thinking I was either senile or crazy. They said not to touch any fish and they were picking up any and all dead wildlife. They said to call the number on their card immediately if I found any dead or dying creatures. She pulled a wet, dirt-stained business card out of her apron pocket. "I knew they'd take Chrissy and probably dump her in a hole or cremate her so I never told them about her."

Quinn's stomach was tied in knots and he was about to break down himself.

"Mrs. Trudeau, I am so truly sorry about Chrissy and the way those agents treated you. I honestly believe there is something really bad going on here. Maybe even a government cover-up." Suddenly a light flipped on in Quinn's mind. He didn't know if he dared ask Mrs. Trudeau, but felt he had to. With an honest but pained voice Quinn asked: "Mrs. Trudeau, I know how much you loved Chrissy, but there may be a way that Chrissy could help us find out what is really going on".

He then explained his ruined plan to get fish samples to someone, hopefully his former girlfriend, to try to analyze them. He told her how he was treated by the Homeland Security agents and how they made him feel like some lowlife. He could tell the fire was rekindling in her eyes. "Mrs. Trudeau, if it's any consolation, her passing might provide a clue to what has happened. She may end up saving all creatures, even human lives, by what we find in her body. I promise you we will treat Chrissy with respect, and I will return her remains to you, and we'll both give her a proper burial."

But her mind was made up before he even uttered those words. "Quinton, take Chrissy with you now and do what you have to do. We're going to make things right."

"Thank you," murmured Quinn softly. He put his arms around her and held her gently for several minutes. Tears flowed freely from both their eyes. She gently picked up the container and handed it to Quinn. She placed a bright red bougainvillea spray over the box and murmured a few parting words in Cajun which Quinn didn't know but understood nonetheless.

Chapter 14 - June 2, 2010 – 9:30 AM

As Quinn walked around Mrs. Trudeau's side yard, he looked both directions to be sure there were no Homeland Security agents combing the area. He quickly headed for home and placed the cake container in the refrigerator turning the temperature down as low as it would go. It occurred to him that, from what he remembered, Chrissy was a good-sized cat, but the cake box felt rather light. The thought didn't register at the moment.

His nerves were frazzled, but he knew he had to make contact with LeAnn right away. He wasn't quite sure how to approach her and really felt awkward calling out of the blue.

Quinn and LeAnn had lived together for two years when he dropped out of junior college. But they eventually realized her goals in life were different than his. While Quinn was content with fishing the bayous, LeAnn moved away to go to Veterinarian school majoring in biology and veterinarian medicine. Strangely, neither one of them had married, Quinn because of what became a rather reclusive life, and LeAnn because of the long hours of study followed by years of building a successful veterinarian clinic.

He had spoken to her several times since then, mostly as friends rather than lovers. It had been over a year since they last talked. After thinking over his words for a few minutes, Quinn decided he should get to the point quickly. He had gotten the clinic phone number from information the night before, so dialed it up right away. The receptionist answered. Quinn asked for LeAnn Roberts, but was told she was in emergency surgery on a dog that had been hit by a car. Quinn asked her to please give LeAnn a message to call him as soon as possible and that it was urgent.

He thought about calling Jesse but didn't want to tie up the phone. He got some coffee and tried to relax. But he was wired up way too tight. Minutes seemed like hours. Finally after thirty minutes the phone rang.

LeAnn said brightly, "Quinn, how are you?" She sounded genuinely glad to hear from him. "I got your message. I hope nothing bad has happened to you. You're not hurt, are you?"

"No, physically I'm fine except for being exhausted. But I have a favor to ask you."

"Ok, shoot," she said, although there was a touch of uneasiness in her voice. She knew Quinn was not one to ask for favors unless something was really wrong.

Quinn proceeded to recap the events of the last two days. After he finished, there was silence on the other end for a moment. "Whew!" she said finally, with air escaping from her lungs like steam from a teapot. "I'm trying to digest what you've told me. My guess is you'd like to have me perform a necropsy on Chrissy to see if I can determine what caused her death."

"Precisely," said Quinn, relieved that he hadn't had to ask directly. "What do you think? Can you do it without notifying anyone else?"

LeAnn thought a minute then answered, "Normally this would be requested by the pet owner, and there are forms to fill out. What condition is the body in?"

"I don't really know," answered Quinn. "I haven't opened the cake saver."

LeAnn almost seemed to be talking to herself out loud, "If there are any suspected infectious diseases, we have to notify the county. I don't want to jeopardize my license or operation of the clinic. But if I suspect there is some new feline disease incubating, a preventative autopsy would be permitted in advance of the paperwork. Where is the body now? I hope you're keeping it cold."

"It's in my refrigerator at the coldest temperature it can crank out. I didn't think I should freeze it."

"That's good." said LeAnn. "If you could drive it up to my office today, I'll stay over and at least have a look at it after hours. What you should do is place the cake saver in a large cooler and pack ice all around it. Then get it here ASAP."

"Thanks so much, LeAnn. You're the best. Please be gentle with the cat because I promised Mrs. Trudeau I'd return Chrissy's remains to her for a proper burial. Oh and please be careful," added Quinn, reminding her about the four disappearing humans in body bags brought back from the leak site.

Chapter 15 - June 2, 2010 – 10:30 AM

Quinn thanked LeAnn again and hung up. He found a box about the right size having to dump out the clothes stored in it waiting for a trip to Goodwill. He suddenly realized he had a lunch appointment with Grace Connelly, the newspaper reporter, in an hour. Quinn nearly panicked. Getting Chrissy to LeAnn's clinic definitely took priority, but he wanted to talk with Grace because she might have access to others he'd never think of that might open doors to the mystery.

He grabbed the phone and prayed that Jesse was home and could make the trip to Baton Rouge. He was about to hang up after the fifth ring when Jesse picked up, breathing like he just finished a 100-yard wind sprint.

"Jesse, man I'm sure glad you're home. Are you working out?"

Jesse laughed, "Nah, I was chopping some wood out back so we'll have it this winter. I was hoping you were one of the guys returning my call concerning doing some investigative work for us. I had to sprint in 'cause I didn't hear the phone at first. Maybe I do need to work out more, especially those wind sprints." Jesse was in better shape than most guys half his age.

"Jesse, getting us some help might have to wait a day or so." I've got a secret mission for you." Quinn described what had happened so far today, and by the time he finished Jesse sounded like he was ready to explode. Jesse nearly jumped through the phone line, "I'm tellin' ya, Quinn, heads are going to roll over this and I'll be the one swingen' the axe."

"Ok, calm down some." Quinn smiled, knowing he felt exactly the same way. "Can you take Chrissy up to Baton Rouge? I'm supposed to meet the newspaper gal for lunch today at 11:30. I'll have the box iced down good so all you have to do is take it to LeAnn's. I decided to use just a cardboard box so it wouldn't look suspicious. But it's good and thick so insulation wise it should be as good as a cooler."

"No problem," said Jesse. "I'll head over to your place in about ten minutes."

Quinn figured he'd have just enough time to shower and change his clothes. After showering, he slipped on a clean pair of jeans and an LSU tee shirt, remembering Grace mentioned she'd taken journalism at one of the LSU satellite branches. He was ready just as Jesse pounded on the door. Quinn couldn't figure out why Jesse never used the door bell, but decided if Jesse came to the house very often he'd have to buy some new heavy duty door hinges.

Quinn handed Jesse the box. "Jesse, I put everything inside one of those large trash bags, so it shouldn't leak through to the box. But just in case, here's a towel to put under the box. You better watch your speed so the cops don't start nosing around."

"Yes Mother," quipped Jesse. "But if anyone asks, I'm just taking some cake to my Grandma."

"Yeah, you really look like Little Red Riding Hood," added Quinn. They both headed out, but went in different directions at the end of the street.

Chapter 16 - June 2, 2010 – 11:20 AM

Quinn made it to the restaurant about ten minutes early, which he hoped would give him some time to collect his thoughts. Grace had suggested a sports bar in town which was pretty rowdy at happy hour but wasn't particularly in favor with the lunch crowd. There were only three guys sitting at the bar and a couple in the second booth from the door. Quinn picked a booth near the back so they'd have some privacy and sat facing the door.

Quinn remembered Grace was quite attractive, and to his own surprise remembered she liked Bud Light. He ordered two hoping she'd be on time so her beer wouldn't get warm. He realized he hadn't been on a date in months. This wasn't really a date, yet he started feeling a bit nervous.

At exactly 11:30, the restaurant door opened and a stunning, stately woman entered. She was about 5'7" and had mid length black hair that seemed to shimmer with the sunlight filtering through the bar windows. Quinn remembered her face, and, although he knew she was in her early fifties, she was beautifully proportioned and could easily pass for thirty-something. She had on a knee-length lavender dress which looked casual yet professional at the same time. A crystal pendant accentuated her bust line, flashing multiple colors as the sunlight ricocheted off in different directions. It also seemed to magnify the glow of her jet black hair. He was not the only one who noticed her, as all three guys at the bar turned around on their bar stools. Quinn noted even the guy with his girlfriend followed her briefly with his eyes, trying not to look too conspicuous.

Quinn stood up and waved casually and Grace met him with a smile and pleasant hand shake.

"I took the liberty of ordering a beer for you. I hope a light beer is still your preference," he said, still feeling a bit intimidated by her good looks.

"Thanks, you remembered," she said, smiling. "How have you been, Quinton? You seemed somewhat evasive when you called. Did you find some long thought to be extinct fish out in the Bayous?" Her tone was almost teasing, and she said it with a twinkle in her dark brown eyes that nearly matched the shine in her hair.

Just then the waitress arrived, so they were momentarily interrupted while they placed their order.

"No," replied Quinn. "I really need to talk to you about something totally different, but much more sinister." The word sinister seemed to get Grace's attention immediately as her smile turned into a quizzical expression.

"I'm not sure where to start," Quinn stated with a bit of a stutter. He wanted to be careful how he explained the happenings of the past few days, but also wanted to be open and at the same time not give her all the information. He wasn't sure whether he could trust her, and didn't want her good looks to cause him to drop his guard and offer information he'd later wish he hadn't. So choosing his words carefully, Quinn told Grace about his initial trips to the leak site and his boat being boarded by Homeland Security. He then explained that he'd heard rumors about four bodies being received at the hospital, and then whisked away again by Homeland Security. He didn't say how he heard of this, but made it seem like he was satisfied that his rumor source was reliable.

It was at this point that Quinn paused and asked Grace if she knew anything about any deaths. Grace seemed totally oblivious to any reports of deaths.

"Quinn, I've been covering some of the oil leak disaster stories, as we all have at the paper. There's so much news at various government and industry levels that one person can't cover it all. But nowhere has there been any mention of deaths. That sounds like a totally unfounded rumor. Are you sure this isn't just your attempt to repay Homeland Security?"

Quinn, astonished at her response, replied sternly, "Grace, I'm not the kind of person to hold a grudge, especially over trivial things like my boat being boarded. In fact, I gave Homeland Security the benefit of the doubt on that."

Grace, replying more pleasantly, "I'm sorry, Quinn. I was just trying to test you to see if you were really being honest. I believe you. But I have not heard a word about any deaths related to the oil spill. There were some people who had respiratory problems from breathing the fumes near the oil spill, but they recovered after a few days. Is there anything else that leads you to believe there is a problem?"

Quinn continued with the fish kill, his run in with the Homeland Security agents again at the beach, and the fish samples being taken away from him. He intentionally left out the part about building a false bottom in the cooler, his conversation with Jesse about getting a private investigator, and taking Chrissy to LeAnn's for analysis. Quinn added to quell any doubts to his story, "At the time I wasn't really sure what I was going to do with the samples, but I guess it doesn't matter now."

When he finished, Quinn summarized by saying, "Grace, something doesn't seem right about this. It's almost like someone is trying to cover up the truth. I was hoping you had some contacts and could poke around, ask some questions, and maybe get some straight answers."

Grace seemed to ponder this for a moment. She hesitated, and then said, "This could be a really big story or nothing at all." But thinking to herself, *if there is a cover-up and I had it first, it would be a career enhancing story.*

She continued, "The fish kill is big news and we reporters were kept what we thought was an unacceptable distance away from the dead wildlife collecting areas. It was for our own safety we were told. As far as I know, no one has really gotten a close-up picture of the remains of the creatures. Actually, you may have been the only one, besides Homeland Security and maybe the police, to see the dead sea life close-up and actually touch them. You didn't get sick."

"No, I didn't, at least not yet," Quinn answered warily, hoping if it was some type of sickness that there wasn't an incubation period involved. "I did have gloves on. But the fish I bagged seemed so much lighter than what a normal fish that size would be." He was about to add that Chrissy seemed light too, but caught himself. A flicker of recognition triggered in his mind that size versus weight might be a clue to something very important. He made a mental note to call LeAnn about this as soon as possible.

Grace finally rubbed her temples, obviously struggling with whether to undertake this challenge. "I may be nuts and regret this," sighed Grace, "but I'll dig some and see what surfaces. I'm thinking maybe I'll try some contacts high up like maybe someone in Senator Lee's office. Perhaps they can shake things up from the political end. Senator Lee is coming up for election next year, and this whole oil spill is going to be a major issue during his campaign. If I can spin this like he would look good being as proactive as possible, I might just be able to get some attention."

Quinn was impressed. *Maybe Grace is a lot tougher than she looks,* he thought. *Many a man has underestimated a good looking woman who turned out to be smart as well as beautiful.* Quinn thanked Grace and asked, "Will you please contact me if you find out anything? I have a vested interest in this issue, as do all of us on the Gulf Coast."

"I will," Grace answered.

They shook hands as they said goodbye. Quinn thought he detected more than just a casual touch. Being short on optimism at the moment, Quinn thought to himself, "that would be my luck. I actually meet an interesting, attractive woman, and we end up with an impending disaster that encompasses all of the Gulf Coast. She'll be consumed by the story and totally forget about me. Well there's always my love of the ocean to fall back on. Of course that's assuming there will be fish left to catch."

Chapter 17 - June 2, 2010 – 4:00 PM

LeAnn Roberts was an accomplished veterinarian that truly loved her work. Her clinic was rapidly becoming the place of choice for both locals and people in neighboring communities. She had expanded her staff, and now handled most every type of pet problem.

LeAnn worked long hours, to the point of almost becoming a workaholic. Although she still had feelings for Quinn, his call from yesterday made her feel uneasy. She was replaying the call in her mind when her clinic phone rang.

She answered quickly, "Roberts Animal Clinic."

Quinn replied, "Hi, LeAnn. It's Quinn. I had some other information I wanted to pass on to you. Did Jesse get Chrissy's body to you?"

"Yes he brought the carton in about 3:00 PM. He didn't stay long because he wanted to consult with one of his Marine buddies on some business idea he had. What did you want to discuss?"

"Well I just wanted to share some observations I noted when I was at the beach trying to get samples. The fish I had picked up was much lighter than I expected based on its size. The fish almost collapsed around my hand when I started to bag it, as if there was nothing inside, even though the skin was intact. Also, Chrissy, which I remembered was a right good-sized cat, seemed to weigh a fraction of what I would have anticipated. I don't know if this means anything, but I thought you should know."

"Thanks for the input Quinn," replied LeAnn with a degree of trepidation. "I'll probably start the necropsy a little after 5:00 PM. Since its Friday, most of the staff will have left by then, and I'll try to close up early unless an emergency comes in."

"Thanks LeAnn. Take care and let me know what you find out."

*****

It was about 5:15 when LeAnn locked up and was ready to begin the necropsy on Chrissy. She set up her tape recorder so she could verbally record what she observed. She removed the cake saver with Chrissy's body from the refrigerator where it was placed when Jesse brought it in. She set the cake saver onto a small metal topped table with a vented hood which removed bad odors that usually accompanied this type of work. The hood vented to the outside, but did have a filtering system to capture any particles or fur that might be released during the dissecting process. She donned a surgical mask and rubber gloves.

LeAnn switched the tape-recorder on but left the vent fan off for the time being. She then carefully began opening the cake saver. Although she had done numerous necropsies, for some reason she felt nervous and apprehensive with this one. It was as if she was half expecting something to explode.

When she began speaking into the recorder, her voice squeaked at first, "June 2, 2010 - 5:15PM. Starting necropsy of a female tabby cat named Chrissy. The cat was delivered from Mrs. Ronald Trudeau of RUE James Street Bayou Cane, Louisiana. The cat died of unknown causes at approximately 4AM today. Concern is that some potentially contagious disease may be involved."

With the cake saver lid removed but not yet touching the cat, LeAnn continued, "There is no apparent external damage to the cat. The fur looks normal with typical color and condition." She reached for her tape measure and checked Chrissy's length. "The cat measures fourteen and one quarter inch in length."

She then lightly moved her hand across the cat's fur, pushing it back to expose the skin. "Skin color appears normal with no lacerations or other abnormalities. There is no evidence of fleas or ticks."

LeAnn began to feel more comfortable with the procedure and wondered if Quinn was maybe overreacting. She remembered him being rather excitable, which did make their sex life enjoyable. She forced herself to push those thoughts away and concentrate on the job at hand.

She then lifted the cat's legs to check the paws for color and condition. This jolted her back to reality because, instead of the expected Riga mortise, the leg moved freely although it felt light and bony. She summarized this in words on the recorder then started to pick up the cat to move her to the weighing table. The cat's body seemed to collapse around her hands like a deflated balloon. LeAnn felt the skeletal bones shifting around her hands. LeAnn was so shocked she almost dropped the cat. Total amazement, then fear gripped LeAnn as a shot of adrenalin cursed through her body. "What the hell?" she shrieked and set the cat back down. Even more astonishing the cat seemed to re-inflate taking up its previous nearly-normal appearance.

LeAnn staggered back a few steps trying to get hold of her emotions. Her heart was racing and she gasped in quick, shallow breaths. After a few moments she started to get control of herself. Speaking out loud for the recorder she summarized what had transpired, then stated, "I am turning the cat over to make an incision in the chest cavity." She delicately cut through the skin making an incision about three inches long.

As she was about to peel back the skin to observe the internal organs, she halted so abruptly she crunched her fingers together cracking her knuckles. A fine mist of tiny reddish brown droplets drifted out through the incision forming a small fog-like cloud slightly above the cat's body. The cloud seemed to hover there. LeAnn was mesmerized unable to speak. Her face contorted with a questioning look of disbelief.

The fog-like mist then started to drift toward her. It was probably propelled by currents of air from the central air conditioner fan which hummed faintly in the background. One of the air vents in the middle of the ceiling was directed toward her.

As if pushed by a higher power, LeAnn reached, seemingly in slow motion, for the hood exhaust fan switch. She was afraid to move too quickly as if her motion might attract the fog. She flipped the switch to the on position. As the hood fan powered up, the cloud, which must have been neutrally buoyant, moved with the air being pulled out by the exhaust fan and disappeared. Thinking back later it was amazing how the turn of a simple switch saved her life.

LeAnn slumped to her knees and beads of sweat trickled into her eyes causing her to blink repeatedly. She wasn't quite sure what to do next but decided not to do anything at least until her hands stopped shaking. After nearly two minutes, she decided she had to look inside the cat. She got to her feet and cautiously approached the body, completely forgetting to recount what had happened on the tape recorder which had been in record mode the entire time.

She began gently squeezing the cat's body at a location away from the incision to see if any additional droplets appeared. None did. She continued this process, gradually working her way toward the incision. When she was satisfied there was no additional danger of fluids that might get on her skin or into her eyes, she reached down and parted the folds of skin.

Aiming the needle point beam of light from her adjustable light source toward the chest cavity, she gasped again with disbelief. The cat's lungs, heart and circulatory system supplying these organs were gone. Most of the muscle tissue adjacent to the organs was also missing. There was no evidence of blood anywhere. LeAnn lengthened the incision to allow inspection of the rest of the body. Most of the stomach was gone. The intestines were simply dangling, not attached to anything. However, the ends of the intestines seemed to be sealed off, which she later decided explained why the fog of droplets didn't simply exit the body through its natural channels.

LeAnn had never seen anything even remotely similar to what she was observing. It was as if something had eaten the cat from the inside out. The cat must have endured extreme pain for whatever time it took until the life was sucked out of her. Tears welled in LeAnn's eyes. "God help us" were the last words she uttered before finally realizing the tape recorder was on, then shutting it off.

Chapter 18 - June 2, 2010 – 6:45 PM

LeAnn carefully placed Chrissy's remains back into the cake saver in case there might be evidence on the cake saver base, snugged the lid, then returned it to the refrigerator. Her mind was numb, not able to comprehend what had just happened, nor what the consequences could be. She flopped into her desk chair trying to force her brain to function logically.

As she struggled mentally, the phone rang angrily making her jump nearly out of her chair. Picking up the receiver, she heard Quinn's voice on the other end, "LeAnn, have you had a chance to examine Chrissy?"

There was no reply. "LeAnn, are you there? Are you all right?"

LeAnn finally managed a weak reply, stuttering, "I… I…I'm ok, I guess."

Quinn could sense the strain in her voice and asked nervously, "What is going on? What happened?"

LeAnn finally gathered herself enough to recount the autopsy. When she finished, there were several moments of silence.

Quinn finally asked, "LeAnn, what does this mean? Could this affect other animals or even humans?"

LeAnn answered wearily, "Quinn, I just don't know. I've never seen anything like it. I should contact the county animal health district so they can review the situation."

Quinn nearly shouted, "No! Please don't do that, at least not yet. Isn't there someone else we could discuss this with? I'm really worried about any level of government getting involved. With all the bureaucracy, it could get tied up for months, and I'm beginning to think we don't have that much time to waste. What happened to Chrissy only took a matter of hours."

LeAnn mulled this over for a few seconds. "Quinn, legally I can't just sit on this. I can't jeopardize my clinic. Let me think about it. Maybe there is someone I could contact who might have a connection, but I need to contact animal health no later than tomorrow morning."

Quinn took a deep breath and then responded, "Ok, I understand. But whoever you contact, please be sure it is someone you can trust. Oh, and LeAnn, thank you for doing the autopsy. I know you are taking a big risk."

Chapter 19 - June 2, 2010 – 7:15 PM

After saying goodbye to LeAnn, Quinn decided to update Jesse and see if he had found a private investigator. Quinn dialed Jesse's cell phone and got him on the second ring. Jesse was really excited and started in before Quinn could say a word, "I found the perfect guy. He was our unit Chaplin in the marines and now is a Baptist minister of sorts."

"Minister, I thought you were getting a private I?" responded Quinn dejectedly. "And what do you mean sort of?"

"Well, his name is Luther Brown. He runs missions for the homeless and disadvantaged. He sets them up and trains people on how to run them. He's got about 10 already, some in each part of the country. He knows people in all walks of life but particularly in the government because he goes after government grants for minority businesses and rehabilitation."

Quinn started to get a little more interested but was still skeptical.

Jesse continued, "But there's another side to Luther. He's a Jeckle and Hyde kind of guy. As a youth, he had a real anger problem and a terrible temper. He grew up in the slums of LA. As a teenager he was getting into drugs and gangs. His mother raised him since his father was a drunk. She knew if Luther continued on the road he was on, he'd probably end up either in jail or killed. So she moved them to

Iowa and forced him into missionary school. That's how he got into religion, and he realized very early that it saved his life."

"The other thing about Luther is he's huge. He's about 6'6" and 370 lbs. I've never seen anyone that big move so fast. He was on the wrestling team in high school and went undefeated every year he was on the team. He won the state heavyweight championship and all the big name wrestling colleges were after him, but he chose to be a minister instead."

"After missionary school, he joined the marines as a Chaplin. While in the marines, he also took up martial arts and soon became an instructor. He's a 4th degree black belt in karate and a master in most of the martial arts. He always wears baggy clothes, and at first glance most people assume he's pudgy and slow. But just a warning, he still struggles with anger management; and if you see his right eye begin to twitch, I strongly recommend you back away a few steps because all hell is about to break loose."

"It was a stroke of luck that I tracked him down. He's setting up a mission near Baton Rouge and was in the capital trying to raise funding. I told him what has transpired so far, and he said he wanted to help. He'd like to meet all of us tomorrow, if possible."

"I'm beginning to like your selection, Jesse," said Quinn. "But do I have a story for you, and it emphasizes why I think this is an urgent situation." Quinn then recounted the autopsy LeAnn had just completed. Jesse was dumbfounded.

"What do you think this means?" he asked.

"I don't know, but we have to find an expert who might have some insight. Would this Luther Brown have any ideas?"

"We can sure ask."

Chapter 20 - June 2, 2010 – 4:00 PM

After Quinn had left Grace Connelly at the sports bar, Grace tried to formulate a plan for some old fashioned investigative reporting. Quinn had made quite an impression on her, and she was honestly concerned about what impact the oil spill could have on all their lives.

Getting back to her office, she tried to address other issues on her calendar, but her thoughts kept returning to Quinn's description of the dead fish and Homeland Security interference. She finally went to her boss, the head editor named Leon. Leon was hard nosed, but Grace had a knack for softening him up. She knocked on his door, which was only partially shut. He was on the phone but waved her in. She sat down in the leather chair facing him. She crossed her legs making sure her dress came to rest slightly above her knees and gave him a sensual smile.

Leon, who was most likely setting up a golf game for the weekend, cleared his throat and said, "Look, Marv, I've got someone in the office so I'll call you back later. See ya." Leon's eyes shifted to Grace's legs then back to her eyes. "Wow, you're looking good. You have a date tonight or did you get dolled up just for me?"

"Now, Leon" retorted Grace, "you know harassment is not tolerated in the work place."

"Come on, Grace," sparred Leon, "I was trying to compliment

you. Besides, I'm sure you're here to weasel something out of me. What's up?"

"As usual, I can't get anything past the master. I've got the makings of a real career- changing story that could put our paper in the limelight. I'd like to devote full time to this at least for a week."

Leon looked at her appraisingly, "Of course you can't tell me what it's about right?"

"Not yet."

Leon scratched his chin. "I'll tell you what. I'll give you three work days, until next Wednesday, to come up with something to convince me why I should let you go full time on this so-called blockbuster story. Don't let me down. Give your other stuff to Mary. Her workload is a little light anyway."

"Thanks, Leon. You're a sweetheart," Grace replied, standing up and giving him a kiss on the cheek.

"Hey, no harassment," barked Leon, loving every minute of it.

Chapter 21 - June 2, 2010 – 4:20 PM

Instead of pushing on the government angle, Grace decided to first check with GG Oil concerning oil sampling. She figured the oil company must be running analysis of the crude oil coming up from the bottom of the ocean, and probably more analysis after the crude oil was mixed with the oil dispersing agents they were using to try to break up the oil.

She looked up the name of the press agent that provided GG's statement to all the news reporters after the fish kill. His name was Carl Frances. She called him, but got his answering machine. She left her name and number, but figured since she didn't represent a major network he'd probably never call back.

Grace then thought a different approach might at least get a real person. She decided to work on a premise that GG wanted favorable PR and would probably do anything to get it. She thought perhaps asking for core sample information to support a junior college archeological paper that Quinn and his amateur group were researching might be a good angle. She tried to call Quinn to let him know of her idea, but couldn't reach him. She decided to wing it.

She went online and got two phone numbers for GG Oil Company public relations. She called them but got an answering machine for both. She again left her name and number. After striking out three times, her enthusiasm was starting to wane.

She then remembered seeing GG Oil adds on TV trying to show how GG was a good neighbor and working diligently to clean up the spill. Her last thought was to call the local TV station WKEL to find out who was in charge of placing the ads. She knew the WKEL marketing manager, Dave Weinstein, and decided a personal visit might get better results. The station was only a 10-minute drive from her office. She grabbed her purse, realizing she better hustle if she was to catch him before he left for the weekend.

Dave Weinstein was on the third floor of a high rise office building on Main Street. Entering the building, Grace was stopped by the receptionist asking if she had an appointment. Grace, of course, did not, but she suggested that Weinstein would definitely want to see her. The receptionist called ahead and Dave sounded eager to see Grace, which she knew he would.

Weinstein was a real womanizer, which was the demise of his first and second marriage. "Some guys just don't get it," Grace smiled to herself. She figured a show of a little cleavage might help distract Dave, so she undid the top few buttons on her blouse, making it look like it just slipped open. She knocked lightly on his door and got an answer to "come on in". His secretary, Mona, was in with him but excused herself as Grace entered. Mona gave Grace a disapproving nod of her head as she passed. Dave on the other hand was all smiles. He did a double take as he watched her enter his office.

"Grace, it sure is great to see you. You look more ravishing each time I see you."

"Dave, you're always working it, aren't you?" she replied with an inviting smile.

"Just being honest," he said, returning her smile with a wink. "To what do I owe the honor?" he asked, not really caring what the answer would be as he was thinking way ahead, like the best way to ask her for a date.

Grace choosing her words carefully, said, "Dave, I'm working on a project with an amateur archeologist named Quinton Jones. I wanted to talk to GG Oil about what they might have found in core samples during drilling of the Deep Horizon well. It would help with the archeological background and we'd put a positive spin on how helpful GG Oil is concerning education. I haven't had much luck contacting their PR people and thought maybe you had a contact since you're running their ads on the clean up."

"Well, you know they're anal about giving out information. But for you maybe I could stretch the rules a little bit. Plus it sounds like good propaganda, and I'm sure they could use some positive PR." With that he got up and headed for his file drawer casually brushing Grace's leg as he passed her chair. She wanted to tell him off right there, but needed the information more than the verbal satisfaction.

Dave pulled the GG Oil file and made Grace a copy of the name and number of the assistant marketing account manager that bought the time spots on TV. Trying to impress Grace, he added, "This has his cell phone direct line, which should bypass any answering machines. They wanted our feedback on viewer reaction so he should answer calls. In fact, he may still be in the area because he mentioned wanting to shoot more videos of local beaches and clean up efforts so they could generate additional adds."

"That's enough about business though," he said with his smooth I'm a nice guy voice. "I just had a great idea. I have some tickets to a dynamite Blues show in New Orleans for this Saturday evening. Are you interested in joining me? I'll have to do some rearranging of plans, but we could spend a nice weekend in the Big Easy."

Grace figured the rearranging of plans meant he already had a date with some other bimbo who maybe wasn't quite as desirable, so he'd have to come up with an excuse why he couldn't go with her. "That does sound inviting, but I only have a few days to convince my editor why this story is worth spending time on. I'm really sorry but I just can't take the time off." Grace said it with just the right expression which wasn't too difficult because it was true, at least partially. Then she added, "Thank you for asking though."

Dave looked genuinely disappointed, but he wasn't one to accept rejection. In his mind it meant he'd keep Grace in the "active dateable file."

Grace had what she wanted and was having trouble not showing her disgust at Dave's creepy come-ons. So she thanked him and put out her hand to shake his. Dave lightly grabbed it and gave the back of her hand a kiss. "Grace, it is always a pleasure. Here's my card if you want to give me a call for any reason." He wrote his home phone on the bottom to cover all the bases.

Grace smiled and thanked him again. As she headed out of his office, Dave called after her, "I'd rather you not mention to GG's assistant manager how you got his number." Grace nodded but thought to herself, "paybacks can be hell."

Chapter 22 - June 2, 2010 – 5:30 PM

After leaving Weinstein's office building, Grace decided to try contacting GG's assistant marketing manager whose phone number Weinstein had just given her. His name was Robert Volker. She dialed up his cell phone number. He answered on the third ring and with a smooth baritone voice replied, "Volker."

Grace trying to be business like and seductive at the same time replied, "Mr. Volker, this is Grace Connelly from the Gulf Coast Times. I was referred to you by WKEL in Baton Rouge, who thought you might like some positive public relations."

Volker replied somewhat cautiously, "Well, Ms. Connelly, we could certainly use good PR right about now. Please elaborate."

Grace continued, "You can just call me Grace. I am trying to put together a piece on how oil drilling can advance geological knowledge through core sampling and such. I'm working with a local amateur archeologist by the name of Quinton Jones. We're really looking for something positive to give our readers." Grace tried to make it sound like they were small town country folk, which in fact was reality, trying to find a nugget of good news in all the horror stories of wildlife dying and environment destruction. She could tell Volker was mulling this over as well.

Finally Volker answered, "Grace, I'll tell you what. I like your approach, and GG really does want to advance education across all disciplines. We are a company that wants to be a good influence on the local communities wherever we do business. If you'd like, we could meet for lunch tomorrow. I'll bring along one of our geologists who can provide some technical expertise."

Grace knew Volker was simply relaying the company line, but at the same time she was excited and thankful that he was willing to discuss this on such short notice. "Thank you so much, Mr. Volker," she said with genuine sincerity. "Would about 12:30 fit your schedule, which I'm sure is extremely busy? I'll take a chance that Mr. Jones is available at that time."

"Sure, that's fine," replied Volker. "Does the Seafood at Sundown Restaurant on the levy sound ok to you?"

"Perfect." She knew that restaurant was very upscale and thought to herself, "big oil never skimps on the perks." She also hoped Quinn wouldn't be too uncomfortable at such a high class place, then realized she had yet to tell Quinn of any of her plans. She thanked Volker again for his time and consideration and then said goodbye.

By now it was nearly 6PM, so Grace tried calling Quinn again. This time she got through. "Quinn," she said excitedly, "I've got some promising news to share."

"I have some news too, but it's definitely not promising. In fact, it's scary. You go first."

Grace re-iterated what she'd done and the 12:30 lunch meeting she'd arranged.

After listening to the details Quinn said appreciatively, "Thanks, Grace. You're amazing. I had no idea how resourceful you are."

Quinn was already feeling bad about not telling her the whole story up front. He continued, "First, I have an apology to make. I left out some details when we first talked." He struggled trying to find the right words, "I wasn't sure ....well, ah.... I just didn't know how much I should tell you."

"You mean you didn't know if you could trust me."

"Yeah. I truly am sorry," he replied dejectedly.

"What did you leave out?" she asked, thinking just maybe she'd been setup and totally wrong about believing Quinn in the first place.

Quinn decided to tell her everything. He told her about Mrs. Trudeau and Chrissy and the autopsy. After hearing the story, Grace knew her original intuition had been dead on, and that this was sounding more and more like a once-in-a-lifetime story.

Chapter 23 - June 2, 2010 – 8:00 PM

After his discussion with Grace, Quinn decided all of them should get together in person to forge out a real plan. They were looking more like a team of misfits, and they were going up against big oil and apparently at least one arm of the federal government. They needed to work together if they were to get anywhere besides ending up in jail. Grace liked the idea and offered her office as a place to meet. Quinn felt pretty sure he could get Jesse and Luther on short notice, but he was most worried about LeAnn.

To his surprise, Quinn was able to convince LeAnn to meet with all of them that evening at 8PM in Grace's office. Everyone was there by 8:15 and Quinn got them started with introductions. Quinn asked LeAnn to give a first-hand account of the autopsy, which she did with precise detail. It seemed like no one took a breath during the description.

After she finished, LeAnn added that she had thought of someone who might be the expert they needed. "I remember a PhD in microbiology by the name of Dr. Winston Edwards who was one of the reviewers of my thesis. I was extremely impressed by his knowledge and honesty, but he was never particularly tactful and said exactly what he was thinking. He always seemed to be at odds with "the establishment" as he called it. He was a rising star in the field, but his ideas and approach to those in management cost him any chance of obtaining the choice grants and research projects."

Grace piped in, "Yes, I remember seeing some articles on him. He was awarded a primo position at MIT supporting a huge government funded research project, but within two years was pulled from the faculty after some disagreement over how a project was to be managed. Last I heard, he ended up at Berkeley as an adjunct professor."

"You're correct," added LeAnn. "He has authored some cutting-edge papers on virus and bacteria interactions. From what I've heard, he reaches conclusions often times bypassing normal substantiation protocol. He's right probably 99% of the time, which drives his managers and peers crazy. However, he made a decision a few years back on a critical program that turned out to be wrong. A lot of money was spent and it took vital time to recover, causing MIT to nearly lose their funding. After that, Dr. Edwards was asked to leave."

"Well, it sounds like he certainly is knowledgeable, but if he finds something, knowing his reputation, would he have enough credibility to get people in charge to take action?" Quinn asked.

Luther spoke up for the first time, "From experience, I know that experts in any field do not come cheap, and I don't think any of us have money to pay someone to do any kind of analysis on Chrissy's remains. Listening to what you all have described, this Dr. Edwards has legitimate credentials, and might just be willing to take this on "pro bono" so to speak. LeAnn, how well do you know him?"

"I've been out of contact with him for a year or more, but I think he'll remember me. I'm willing to try to persuade him to help us."

"Ok," Quinn said. "Our plan as I see it would have three parts. We need a detailed expert analysis of what happened to Chrissy. Second, we need to know what GG Oil has been doing concerning analysis of the crude oil and how it might be reacting with sea life. Finally, I'd certainly like to know how Homeland Security is involved and what their investigation has determined." Everyone nodded in agreement. "I think we should give LeAnn part one since she has first-hand knowledge and a possible expert in mind." Everyone agreed.

"The second part would be to try to get information from GG Oil on what exactly is going on from a crude oil sample analysis basis." Quinn asked Grace to go over what she'd set up for tomorrow.

Grace summarized her discussion with Robert Volker. After she finished, Luther spoke again, "I suspect GG will be reluctant to give out much information, but perhaps the geologist might offer something that we could follow up on. I'd pump him as much as possible without making them too suspicious. Plus, we might need Grace's journalistic contacts as a trump card at some point." Both Quinn and Grace were gaining more respect for Luther's opinion each time he spoke.

"Ok, Grace and I will take on part two," responded Quinn.

"I have something in mind for part three," offered Luther. "I'm scheduled to have a meeting with Senator Lee on Monday concerning funding for my mission here in Louisiana. I'll move the conversation toward Homeland Security's involvement. I have some contacts that might provide a little leverage on getting to the real story. Jesse and I will work that end."

Jesse, who had been quiet, finally managed a smile. Jesse related the story of what had happened at the hospital with the four bodies. It seemed way more than a day ago. "My wife Ginger has tried to find out more details, but that trail is stone cold."

"That tidbit might just give us some of that leverage I just mentioned," Luther said smiling.

"Sounds like we've got a plan," Quinn said. "Let's hope we can get some results."

With that everyone shook hands.

"Why don't we call our group the "Tidal Surge?" offered Grace.

"We might need a Tsunami to wash this thing out in the open," joked Luther. That would prove to be an understatement.

PART TWO

Chapter 24 - May 6, 2010 – 9:00AM

During the days leading up to the formation of the "Tidal Surge Group" as Grace called them, Beauregard Calhoun had been on a different mission. He was formulating a plan to ensure that "his land" would become available to fill his lifelong dream of a Southern Plantation theme park unrivaled anywhere. After scheming in his own mind for several days, Beau placed a call to Senator Clarence Lee's personal phone line.

"Clarence," voiced Beau in his smoothest southern drawl, "how are you this fine day?"

Senator Lee, sensing something must be up for Beau to call unannounced, replied heartily, "I couldn't be better unless I had a mint julep in one hand and a fine southern belle on my lap."

"Well, both could be arranged," laughed Beau, knowing there was more than a kernel of truth in Lee's comment.

"Well, Beauregard," said Lee, "I'm sure you didn't call just to discuss my health and wellbeing for the day. What's on your mind?"

"Senator, we both know the race for your seat was pretty tight last election, and the fallout from this damn oil leak is not looking good. I'm thinking we better gin up a collateral damage plan right quick or you might be one of the casualties."

"My staff and press secretary have been discussing various

scenarios precisely on this topic," answered Lee with a degree of annoyance.

"You mean you weren't even going to consult with good ole' Beauregard for his spin on the situation?" mocked Beau.

"All right, my bet is you have a scheme already in mind with some favors to go with it. So let's get down to it."

"My, my, Senator." chuckled Beau. "You do seem a bit testy for such a fine day. What I had in mind was me organizing a united front with Alabama, Mississippi, and Florida, similar to what we did for the national election. Except this time I'll aim to get federal relief funding, off the books of course, in exchange for votes on critical agendas the White House has. There will be behind-closed-door negotiations involved, for which I have a backlog of unclaimed favors to bargain with."

Senator Lee smiled to himself, knowing Beau had access to unpleasant information various high ranking officials would definitely prefer stay private. "Beau, I'm sure you're proposing most of this out of the kindness of your heart, but there must be a slight catch. I'm guessing you're about to share that with me."

"Ah, Senator, your charm and perception impress this humble servant, as it has your many constituents."

"Cut the bull, Beau," Lee said angrily. "What the hell do you want in return?"

"Do you recall the Louisiana Bayou parcel of land that was placed on the state protected list about 20 years back?"

"Vaguely, I remember you've mentioned it on occasion. Some sort of pet project of yours, right?"

"Yes, that's it. I'd like to have it removed from the list. Then have the land granted to me, at fair market value, of course."

"I'm guessing that fair market value is pretty low about now with the oil spill expected to screw up all the marshes there."

"It truly is a pity how things work out sometimes," declared Beau.

"That doesn't seem to be too unreasonable a price for what you're proposing," Lee stated, feeling suddenly better about their exchange. "There must be something else, or are you just getting soft and cuddly in your old age?"

"I'll want some relaxation of building codes eventually, but we can discuss that later," Beau replied.

"Ok, we have a deal. I'll get land management working on this tomorrow."

Chapter 25 - May 6, 2010 – 10:00 AM

After hanging up with Senator Lee, Beau smiled to himself. His plan was finally coming together. But he also knew politician's promises were about as trustworthy as a nearly dead car battery on a cold day, and that Mother Nature could be extremely finicky. He hadn't become a billionaire by relying solely on someone's word or leaving things to chance. He always had a back-up plan that he personally put into motion, and this was exactly his strategy today.

To neutralize Mother Nature, Beau wanted to be sure crude oil would devastate "his land" even if the oil spill didn't reach it naturally. He had arranged for the procurement of two well-used tugboats and a small ocean-going barge through a rather unscrupulous middleman named Dickson. For the right price, Dickson could get anything, and equally important, not leave a paper trail. He made a call to Dickson, finalizing the transaction.

Next, through several other questionable contacts he had, Beau hired two captains to run the boats and set up with a jobber to select a skeleton crew of four seamen to man the boats. Beau specified he wanted illegal aliens that would not ask questions and disappear as soon as the job was completed. Beau insisted that the crews be capable of working around the clock, and for that they'd be paid $200 per hour. Each captain would get paid $300 per hour plus a $2000 bonus if the job was completed on schedule. Beau had long since learned if you wanted a job done correctly, you didn't scrimp on wages.

Beau also asserted that it should be implied to the men that there would be equally profitable additional work. His intent was to keep them focused on following his instructions precisely so they would try to impress him and be in-line for future work. He really had no intention of ever contacting them again.

Beau's plan was to rig the barge with specially-made skimmers and centrifugal separator pumps such that he could capture crude oil on or near the ocean surface. He could then have the crew pass the slurry of crude and sea water through the separators removing most of the sea water, then pump the reclaimed crude into 55-gallon drums. With the small ocean-going barge he could easily store 100 drums and another 50 between the two tugs. This would give him over 8,000 gallons of crude oil with which to spray "his land" just in case the oil spill never reached it naturally.

*****

By May 12 the tugs and barge were outfitted and the crews trained and ready. The rated capacity was 110 gallons of reclaimed crude oil per hour per pumping system. With both systems operating they figured it would take about 38 hours to fill their complement of 150 drums.

Once the drums were filled they would return, but their return destination was not the port from which they left. Instead, they were to return by cover of night to a secluded Bayou in the middle of the land Beau proposed to buy for his theme park. There was a little-known channel that had sufficient draft at high tide to bring the tugs and barge inland to a point where tall cypress and heavy undergrowth could hide the barge. They'd then transfer the 50 drums from the two tugs to the barge which, along with flooding of some of the ballast tanks, would be enough weight to ground the barge until the time came to use the oil. If not needed, they would just let the barge, along with its cargo, rust into oblivion.

The final chapter of the plan was for the two tugs to head to "dead port" which was the nautical scrap yard for the area. Any trail of where the tugs had been would go down with the ships so to speak. With travel time to and from the site included, Beau figured the job should be completed in a week or less.

Since every manner of vessel was being pressed into service by various government entities, there was no issue of being questioned on what they were doing or on whose authority. But just in case, Beau had special work papers drawn up and signed by GG Oil's primary law firm Johnson, Masters & Clark. Beau had close ties with Chip Masters, one of the partners.

To cover the chance that Senator Lee did not follow up with his end of the bargain, Beau planned a separate meeting with James Simmons, the Southeast Regional Director of Homeland Security. Simmons was also someone Beau knew quite well. Beau planned to work that end as soon as his oil reclamation boats were underway.

Chapter 26 - May 14, 2010 – 11:00 AM

The master plan was to have the tugs embark May 13. However, Mother Nature made her first appearance with severe thunderstorms and water spouts in the vicinity of the "Logan Slick", the largest of the oil slicks, which was where they planned to obtain their crude oil. By late morning of May 14, the weather front had moved inland and the tugs, with the barge in tow, headed toward the oil slick which was now approximately 100 miles offshore.

By 9:00 PM they had reached the oil slick, but to their surprise it seemed much smaller than what they had been led to believe. In addition, the ocean's surface seemed to give off a faint, pulsing glow which really freaked out the crew. Although they were hardened seamen, they were also a superstitious lot. Were they not being paid so handsomely, they would have all gladly left immediately.

By 9:30 the barge was in position and the crude oil reclamation was underway. Unknown to any but a few people at GG Oil and the Department of Defense, this was about 38 hours after this slick had been sprayed with the secret OxiMax dispersal agent.

The crude oil reclamation went smoothly and all 150 of the metal 55-gallon drums were filled without incident by 10:00 PM on May 16th. The men had been instructed to follow safety precautions to the letter. They had handled the equipment using safety gloves, smocks, and eye goggles. Specially designed valving in the pump transfer system managed to avoid all spillage when moving the fill lines from drum to drum. Captains Lodaire and Braun were proud of their teams, and could see the big dollar payoff was close at hand. At least so they thought.

Each captain had a special satellite communication link that connected indirectly to Beau via a special disposable cell phone. The captains were only to make three, three-way calls, and were to agree between them prior to making each call. The first was when they completed filling of the drums and were ready to return. The second was when they had reached their return destination and properly grounded the barge. The third was only to be made in an absolute emergency, and depending on the circumstances, could result in the cancellation of their bonuses. That was a call all of them decided would not be made.

After securing all the drums with nylon straps, both captains were ready to make the first call. It was 11:00 PM and the captains dialed up the mutually agreed upon number. They used a prearranged code word "Starbright" which meant they were loaded and ready to begin the return voyage. If there were any further instructions, they would be contacted by return call within ten minutes. The ten minutes passed, they fired up the tugs' engines, and set course by their global positioning radar.

Beau had received the call and smiled to himself. His plan was on track.

Chapter 27 - May 16, 2010 – 11:15 PM

With the tugs more heavily loaded and the barge running deeper in the water due to the extra weight of its cargo, the return trip would take longer. However, that had been factored into the time table. It was critical for the team to reach the bayou channel at high tide. If they missed it, the captains knew they'd have to wait for the next high tide. That would increase the chance of being spotted, even though the location was far away from normal shipping lanes and most pleasure boat traffic.

By 1:00 AM on May 17th the weather turned bad. Another front was moving through and with it came high waves and violent thunderstorms. Knowing their bonuses were in jeopardy, both captains agreed not to alter course to avoid some of the worst storm cells. Both tugs were attached to the barge with tow wires. A single tug could do the tow, but both were being used in case one of them had a mechanical malfunction. Plus, they could make better time. By 2:00 AM Captain Lodaire felt they made a mistake and if nothing else should reduce speed to minimize the pounding on the tugs and the barge. Captain Braun seemed possessed and would not even consider slowing down.

By about 2:30 AM winds were nearing gale force. Whether wind, wave action, or weakened wire strands were the cause, it really didn't matter. Like a gunshot crack, Captain Braun's tow cable snapped, sending the long portion sweeping across the deck of Captains Lodaire's tug nearly cutting one fifty-five gallon drum in two and smashing a large gash through the wall of a second drum. It narrowly missed beheading one of the crewmen named Chavez. Crude oil from the damaged drums spread across the deck. Worse yet, the cable went overboard and got fouled in the tug's prop. Captain Lodaire tried to disengage the transmission, but reacted a split second too slowly. A horrible screeching sound and explosive-like crack announced a drive shaft failure. The tug went dead in the water.

For a moment it looked like the momentum of the barge might send it crashing into the disabled tug probably sinking it on the spot. Fortunately, the wind and waves managed to veer the tug enough that the barge missed it by several feet.

Just as suddenly the wind started to die down, and the buffeting of the waves slackened. This was fortunate since without power the tug was at the mercy of the waves which moments before had threatened to breach the craft. Captain Braun pulled alongside and asked Rodriguez, one of his crew, to transfer to Lodaire's boat to help with the clean up. Some of the crude from the punctured drums had splashed onto Chavez's face and legs although he was happy to be alive after his close encounter with the flailing tow cable. The other seaman on Lodaire's tug, named Jamal, had tried to help Chavez but slipped on the oily deck and smacked his leg on one of the large anchor cleats. He had a nasty gash on his leg and was covered in crude oil where his pants had been ripped. Rodriguez slipped himself when boarding the boat, ripping his shirt when he went down and covering his arm with crude oil.

Captain Lodaire came down from the wheelhouse to survey the damage. He brought a first aid kit and began wiping down Jamal's leg to dress the wound. Since Lodaire had been piloting the tug, he did not have on the deck hands safety gear and made a fatal mistake by not immediately donning the surgical gloves in the first aid kit.

The men washed down the deck so they could move around safely, then re-tightened the nylon straps to make sure they wouldn't lose any more of the oil drums. After about 30 minutes, they finally got around to cleaning themselves up and removing their oil-soaked clothes. A check in the engine room verified their worst fears. The boat would not be moving anytime soon. They put out a drift anchor to keep the boat heading into the seas in case additional storms came up.

The two captains agreed that they would replace the tow cable on Braun's boat and he would continue towing the barge to their rendezvous site. Meanwhile, Lodaire's crew, along with the addition of Rodriguez from Braun's boat, would attempt to repair the stricken tug. The captains also agreed that the third emergency call was not justified; although they would be short the 25 drums, now down to 23, of crude oil still on Lodaire's boat. It would take too much time to attempt to transfer the drums, not to mention the concern for more injuries.

It took about two hours of rigorous work to replace the cable. With that completed Braun powered up and headed for the Bayou site. Braun now only had one crewman named Gomez still on board. Lodaire decided to let the men on his boat rest a couple of hours.

Captain Lodaire set his alarm to be awakened in two hours then quickly fell into a deep sleep. He was jolted awake by intense screaming from the aft deck. His alarm was going off which he thought at first may have been what awoke him as part of a bad dream, but the dreadful shriek repeated again. Lodaire groggily headed for the aft deck where he found Jamal writhing in pain. Rodriguez was by his side.

"What the hell is going on?" Lodaire asked urgently.

"The scream woke me up and I find him like this" answered Rodriguez with a look of terror in his eyes. "I not feel so good either. Maybe something in dat damn oil. Dat eerie light like thing a bad omen."

Lodaire bent down to look at Jamal's leg wound which he thought might be the source of the pain. Jamal shook his head stammering "Not there, not there." He grabbed at his chest. "Inside here," he yelled, then screamed again.

Lodaire was at a loss of what to do. As he started to stand up, he realized that he felt sort of woozy. The other two men, Rodriguez and Chavez didn't look like they felt good either and they were scared. All four of them were tough, hardened men but something was definitely wrong here, something they had never encountered before.

Suddenly Chavez doubled over in excruciating pain. He slumped to the floor next to Jamal whose entire body was now twitching uncontrollably. Chavez trembled in fear and pain and started praying in Spanish. Rodriguez gazed at Lodaire with a probing fearful look.

"Try to make them as comfortable as you can," uttered Lodaire in a near whisper. "I'm going to go call for help."

By the time Lodaire got to the wheelhouse, he was feeling strange. There was pressure building inside his abdomen and his chest felt like it was being squeezed. He called Beau's prearranged number for an emergency and left a message that his tug was dead in the water and now had a medical emergency. He thought at least two of his men might be dying. He was having trouble concentrating but was able to give his latest coordinates. Waves of intense pain greeted him as he flipped off the cell phone. He wanted to issue a mayday call on the radio but wasn't sure he could reach it. He lunged for it and thought he might have caught the "on" switch. He yelled, "Mayday! Mayday!" but was overcome with pain before he could give his call letters. All he could do was scream, then wait for the next wave of pain.

Rodriguez on the aft deck heard the screams from the captain. The other two men had ceased uttering those horrible sounds a minute or so ago and had either passed out or worse. He had lost track of time in this hell. He started to move toward the wheelhouse to help the captain, but before he took two steps the waves of pain began. He staggered a few more feet to the aft storage cabinet where he knew a handgun was kept. He decided he'd rather end this nightmare with a bullet to his head rather than endure the pain his fellow crewmen went through. He managed to get the gun which was kept loaded, but the waves of pain increased beyond his brain's ability to function properly. He got off one wild shot missing himself completely. He fell to the deck of what, only in a matter of minutes, had become a ghost ship.

*****

Beau was having a late dinner when the call came in. The message was somewhat incoherent, but he got the gist of it. He immediately called the reply number which was supposed to go to both captains. Only Captain Braun picked up. Braun summarized what had happened up to the point where he left Lodaire. He knew nothing of the medical emergency, but had picked up a faint mayday call over the emergency radio channel. It wasn't repeated and the required ID was missing, so he had ignored it as either a prank or a radio frequency test.

Braun related that he was making pretty good time and hoped to make the next high tide. He did caution that it might take somewhat longer to position and ground the barge because he was short one crewman. Beau agreed, thanked him for his hard work, then hung up.

Beau was not happy with the turn of events, but felt the overall plan would recover. He did decide to call Simmons from Homeland Security to get a boat out there fast before someone else stumbled onto Lodaire's tug. He didn't want Lodaire or his crew spilling their guts to the wrong people. Little did he know that their guts had already disappeared.

Chapter 28 - May 18, 2010 – 8:10 AM

B eau had called James Simmons, the Southern Regional Director of Homeland Security, shortly after Beau's two tugs and barge headed out to the crude oil slick. He had convinced Simmons it was in the countries, and more importantly, Simmons own best interest to become personally involved. He suggested to Simmons that he could get great political exposure for himself and their department. Plus, Beau offered some of the land he didn't have yet as a secret site to nab drug traffickers using the Bayous as a receiving area for drugs from Columbia and Mexico. Beau also suggested Al Quida might be using the area as a staging site to infiltrate Muslim extremists into the USA. Simmons could see the political advantages, plus he knew Beau had some other unpleasant information on him that suddenly could become public if he resisted. He was actually sold on the idea without Beau even having to play his trump card.

Beau was not planning on needing Simmons so soon, but after getting the emergency call from Lodaire and talking to Braun, Beau called Simmons on his personal line.

"Director Simmons, this is Beauregard Calhoun. How are you today?"

"I'm good so far," Simmons answered with a degree of trepidation. "To what do I owe the honor?"

"Do you recall our conversation a couple days ago concerning your involvement with the oil spill issue?" queried Beau.

"Of course." replied Simmons. "I thought you had some very appropriate ideas."

"Well, I got word from my personal boat captain that there was a strange tug boat in the vicinity of the Larson Oil Slick. It had what appeared to be some sort of contraband in fifty-five gallon drums on board and the crew looked like illegal aliens. My captain had heard rumors that there might be stolen nuclear reactor rods being smuggled into the country, and he was concerned that this information get to someone who could take action." Beau wanted to spool up Simmons with some juicy bait. He accomplished just that.

"Jesus Christ," roared Simmons. "The FBI got word of some potential plot to assemble and detonate a dirty A Bomb in one of our big cities. This could be the critical element of that plan."

"Perhaps you could get a boat out there to investigate and apprehend the crew for interrogation," suggested Beau. "You blow open this conspiracy, and there's no telling where it could take you," he added for extra emphasis.

By now Simmons was salivating. Simmons noted, "I'll do better than that. I'll have some agents fly out there ASAP. Do you have last known coordinates?"

Beau gave him the coordinates Braun had supplied from his GPS.

"Thanks for the tip. I owe you one." With that Simmons hung up.

Beau felt pretty proud of himself. "This might actually turn out better than my original plan," Beau said out loud. It occurred to him that he might even save having to pay Lodaire and his crew, which brought an even bigger smile to his face. "Life is good," he boasted.

Chapter 29 - May 18, 2010 – 8:15 AM

G G Oil's crude oil containment division was stretched to the limit. They had responsibility for trying to cap the leaking well, contain the oil after it reached the ocean surface, and any efforts to chemically break down or eliminate the oil slicks after they formed. Since crude was continually belching from the broken wellhead, it was a monumental task. Breaking down the oil slick was a number three priority. GG's chemists decided to wait at least 72 hours after spraying the OxiMax dispersant before taking samples from the Larson Slick. Experience had shown that it took that long for previous chemicals to provide measurable results, given the size of the slick.

Jake Spencer was the lead on-site chemical engineer. He and his team of three other chemists had been getting samples from the wellhead area when they were notified to head for the Larson Slick for sampling. It would take nearly a day to get to the present location of the slick. In route they compared satellite photos taken late that afternoon with photos from two days ago. To their surprise, the slick covered only about half the area it had previously. This was certainly a positive sign that the OxiMax dispersant was working.

They planned on getting samples at first light before the heat of the day set in. As dawn broke, they noted the slick seemed even smaller. As they were about to begin sampling, the captain, Mike

Miller, called Jake and said he spotted a tug boat about a quarter mile from them, which appeared to be adrift. Mike suggested they at least try to hail the craft. Jake came up to the bridge and took a look through the captain's binoculars. He couldn't see any activity on board the other vessel. The captain had been unable to get a reply by radio.

Jake asked the captain, "Should we take a closer look?"

"I think we should," answered Miller. "They might have some mechanical problem. It sure is unusual for a tug boat to be this far out to sea without a tow."

They pulled to within fifty yards and tried to get a response by speaking over their boat's loud speaker. They heard nothing. As they got closer in, they saw the four bodies.

"I'm going to call the Coast Guard," Captain Miller announced with an unusual note of concern in his voice. "I don't think we should board the tug without direction from the Coast Guard. We don't know what we're dealing with."

Miller put in an urgent "assistance needed" call by radio. The Coast Guard Cutter Reliance responded. After Miller described what they saw, Reliance's commander, Commander Pickens, said he'd launch the cutter's medivac helicopter which could be there within the hour. He said to hold tight until they arrived. Jake's team and Miller's crew were all abuzz with excitement. Jake and Captain Miller decided the sampling could wait until after the Coast Guard arrived.

In about 50 minutes they heard the whup…whup…whup of the approaching helicopter. The helicopter made a slow pass over the scene then hovered over the tug, surveying the situation. In about a minute two men appeared at the side door of the helicopter and were lowered by sling onto the tug's deck. After taking photographs of the positions of the bodies, aerial stretchers were lowered and the bodies hoisted into the helicopter one by one. The entire process took only about 20 minutes.

Meanwhile, Miller was in communication by radio with the chopper. He gave the names of all on board his boat and was told the chopper was going to fly the bodies back to the Reliance where they could be kept in cold storage until they got further direction. The cutter was already in route to their location and would be towing the tug back to port. The chopper pilot relayed from the cutter commander that the GG team could return to their sampling and would be in contact should they need further information.

The big Coast Guard helicopter picked up altitude, then turned and headed southwest. Miller looked at Jake and said, "That sure told us a lot."

"I guess we don't have a need to know," Jake answered sarcastically.

The crew took about 20 minutes preparing for the sampling. They were about to head to the first sampling point, which they identified by coordinates for documentation purposes. As they started up the boat's engines, another helicopter appeared heading directly toward them from the exact opposite direction the Coast Guard helo had headed just 30 minutes earlier.

This was a much smaller helicopter fitted with pontoons which allowed it to land in the water if the seas weren't too rough. As the chopper flew over them, they noted it had Homeland Security emblazoned in large white letters on the belly of the craft. The chopper circled the tug which was only about 50 yards away, then returned hovering over them. One of the helicopter's crew leaned out the side door with a megaphone and ordered, "Do not move your boat or we will fire on you and disable your engine."

"What the hell," cursed Miller slamming his fist on the control panel. He cut the engines and added, "This is fucking ridiculous."

The Homeland Security chopper landed a few yards off their port, lowered a small military style inflatable, and two men began motoring toward them. It must have been powered by an electric motor since it was essentially noise free. The two men approached with guns drawn.

"Jesus Christ," exclaimed Jake. "All I wanted was some oil samples. I wasn't expecting a gun battle."

"I'm agent Harbaugh with Homeland Security," barked the taller of the two men. "Who are you and what are you doing here? Is anyone on board your boat part of the crew from this tug?"

"I'm Captain Mike Miller," answered Miller. "We're employed by GG Oil to take crude oil samples from the oil slick. We called the Coast Guard when we spotted this tug with bodies on their aft deck."

"Bodies?" asked Harbaugh with a look of surprised agitation. "How many and where are they?"

"You're about 20 minutes too late," replied Miller. "The Coast Guard Helicopter plucked them off the deck and headed for the Cutter Reliance. You can radio Commander Pickens to verify our story."

"Our radio isn't frequency-compatible with theirs," replied Harbaugh, now obviously pissed off.

"That figures," snickered Jake under his breath.

"Did you or the Coast Guard check any of those drums for content?" questioned Harbaugh.

"We weren't invited on board, and we didn't see anyone else check the drums," Miller replied. "We were told the cutter Reliance was headed here to take the tug under tow."

"I'm coming on board to check your papers," exclaimed Harbaugh.

"Are you asking permission, which would be the proper etiquette?" asserted Miller now agitated himself.

"No, I'm telling you." Harbaugh stated. "If you're thinking of resisting, I'll quarantine your boat and all on board. You'll spend a pleasant week in the brig on shore. Strictly bread and water rations I'm told." A crooked smile spread across Harbaugh's face.

"Permission granted," Miller said with a shrug of his shoulders.

After coming on board and reviewing Miller's manifest and other assorted paperwork, Harbaugh was satisfied they were telling the truth. He finally told Miller he could proceed with the sampling.

"You know," taunted Miller. "You're the second person who's told me that in the last two hours and I have yet to move from this spot."

The irony was lost on Harbaugh and he matter-of-factly replied, "Not my problem." He and the other agent returned to the tug.

"Well I guess we're finally back to where we started about four hours ago," stated Miller to no one in particular. "We better head out before someone else show's up."

It was now nearing midday. As they approached the location where they were to start sampling, the oil slick was nowhere in sight. They rechecked the coordinates and found them to be accurate. They decided to proceed with the sampling per their instructions from the home office.

The sampling process involved dipping sterile sample bottles into the water, submerging them no deeper than ½ an inch for surface samples. This was all done mechanically so as not to contaminate either the sample bottles or the sample itself. They also took samples at various depths including 1 foot, 5 feet, 10 feet, 20 feet, and could go down to several hundred feet if needed. The 20-foot sample appeared to have a slight discoloration, suggesting that the dispersant had broken down the oil with the concentration of minute particles the highest at the 20-foot depth. Chemical analysis to be done later would have to verify this observation. They then proceeded to the next location and repeated the process. After completing sampling at six different locations, which moved them more and more toward what had been the center of the oil slick, the team was beginning to believe the slick had been completely dissipated, at least down to a depth of 20 feet.

This was extremely exciting and exactly what GG Oil had hoped the new dispersant would accomplish. The team continued sampling, but each subsequent location further substantiated their results. When they completed sampling at all the designated locations, Jake radioed his supervision with the preliminary results. The managers literally pounced on the opportunity to finally have a game-changing breakthrough. This could mean the looming expense of hundreds of millions of dollars for environmental cleanup might be avoided. This could save the company.

Jake warned that subsurface concentrations of oil might still be present and the impacts to sea life still had to be evaluated. But those warnings fell on deaf ears. If the slick was out of sight, it would be out of mind, or so they hoped.

Chapter 30 - May 19, 2010

Over the next several days Homeland Security and the Coast Guard argued over jurisdiction. It was finally agreed that the Coast Guard would do the investigation of the contents of the drums with Homeland Security participation. The decision on investigation of the bodies was still being discussed at higher levels. Both Senator Lee and Regional Director Simmons were personally involved. However, it was determined that no autopsies would be performed until the bodies were transferred to an appropriate facility. The Coast Guard was happy to unload this political hot potato to local authorities on shore and let them battle it out from there.

As the tug was being towed toward shore, special test equipment was flown to the Cutter Reliance. Portable Xray and ultrasound units were ferried in and set up on the tug. The plan was to attempt to "see" inside the drums without opening them. This was accomplished and to everyone's surprise and disappointment, it was determined that there was nothing in the drums except an organic liquid, most likely oil. They also verified there was no radioactivity emanating from the drums. Since it was now concluded there were no drugs, nuclear material, or explosives inside, the urgency of the situation diminished. It was decided that the actual chemical analysis of the liquid could be determined later once they reached their base on shore.

*****PART THREE*****

Chapter 31 - June 4, 2010 – 9:00 PM

After the initial meeting of the "Tidal Surge" LeAnn Roberts headed home. She knew it was two hours earlier on the West Coast, so she decided to try to contact Dr. Edwards in Berkeley. To her surprise an actual person answered her call. It was a graduate student assisting Dr. Edwards. LeAnn found out that Dr. Edwards had gone to Las Vegas for the weekend. She left both her cell phone and the clinic phone number, and asked the grad student to please leave an urgent message that Dr. Edwards call her, regardless of the time.

The next morning LeAnn felt she had to inform the county animal care authorities of a potential infectious feline disease in the Bayou Cane region. The county animal care offices were closed for the weekend so she left a phone message and expected she wouldn't hear anything until Monday morning. She hoped that would give her time to speak with Dr. Edwards.

LeAnn started jotting down some notes on what to say to Dr. Edwards. As she struggled with her thoughts, she was rudely interrupted by her cell phone ringing. The voice on the other end stated rashly, "I understand you performed a necropsy on a cat from the Bayou Cane region and suspect some potential infectious disease. Please provide me the details."

LeAnn couldn't believe what she was hearing and glanced at the clock. It had only been slightly over an hour since she had left the message with county animal control. "Who am I speaking to?" she responded with a concerned voice.

"This is special agent John Barlow of Homeland Security. We are quarantining all wildlife from that area that died after May 25. Do you know the time and date of death?"

"Yes, the cat died yesterday," LeAnn answered cautiously.

"My orders are to confiscate all wildlife remains immediately," asserted Barlow. "Where and when can I meet you to accomplish that? This is a serious matter and requires your complete cooperation, Ms. Roberts."

LeAnn was visibly shaken. She was fearful that they'd shutdown her clinic and maybe even detain her. "I performed the necropsy at my clinic and can be there in about half an hour." she said nervously. "Do you need directions?" she asked.

"No, in fact I'm there now, so the sooner you can be here the better," declared Barlow.

LeAnn suddenly felt nauseous. "Ok," she managed to blurt out. Before she could say anything else, Barlow hung-up.

How the hell could they have gotten the call and responded so fast she thought. She realized how Quinn must have felt when they stopped him on the beach. She decided not to change out of her jean shorts and top, grabbed her purse, and hurried out the door. She thought of calling Quinn but figured he and Grace were probably preparing for their scheduled interview with the GG Oil people. She hoped things would go better for them.

When she arrived at the clinic, LeAnn spotted the brown Buick Sedan waiting in the reserved parking spot with her name on it. She remembered Quinn's comment that they seem to go out of their way to annoy the person they're dealing with. "Probably some psychological strategy they're taught she thought to herself. Ok, just keep your cool," she reminded herself.

As she approached the car, a middle-aged man about 5'10" got out. "I'm agent Barlow," he said with a slight nod of his head. "I'm assuming you're Ms. Roberts."

LeAnn noticed her picture on the seat of his car which had partially slid out of Barlow's file folder. "Yes," she answered, "but I think you knew that already. Do you have files on everyone or just interesting people?" LeAnn said sarcastically.

"Ma'am, generating personal files is routine when we're conducting investigations," replied Barlow. "Can we go inside?"

"May I please see some identification?" LeAnn asked.

Barlow pulled out his badge with a look of displeasure on his face like LeAnn was rude for even asking.

LeAnn headed for the door trying not to look too intimidated, but dropped her office keys while attempting to unlock the door.

Barlow picked them up and handed them to her with the first evidence of a smile. "Can I help with that?" he asked menacingly.

"No thanks. I've got it," LeAnn answered knowing, she'd already lost her composure.

As they went inside, LeAnn tried to recover by asking, "You mentioned an investigation. What are you investigating that would involve a dead cat?" She discerned Barlow hesitating, trying to compose a reasonable answer.

"We're collecting all sick or dead wildlife from the Bayou Cane area because of the oil spill. There's concern from everyone that contact or even breathing the fumes from the crude oil might affect the health of many different organisms. We want to put that concern to bed." answered Barlow.

"What have you found out so far? Is there a problem?" questioned LeAnn.

"We're still in the data collection mode," Barlow replied vaguely. "Did you find anything unusual when you examined the cat?" asked Barlow trying to regain control of the conversation.

"Yeah, its insides were gone," LeAnn responded bluntly.

With that comment Barlow flinched. "I...I'm not sure I understand."

"The cat looked normal on the outside, but when I cut her open to determine the cause of death, most of the internal organs were," she hesitated for effect, "they were gone, seemingly consumed by something." LeAnn purposely left out the part of the strange fog that emanated from Chrissy when she made her initial incision.

Barlow blinked several times. "I'll need to take the cats remains with me for analysis."

"You can't," she blurted, not giving herself time to think properly. "I mean, you have to get county animal control's approval to remove anything from my clinic."

"Ms. Roberts, I have a blanket release from the state that permits me to obtain any evidence, plant, animal, or otherwise, needed to conduct this investigation. Please get me the remains now."

LeAnn took a deep breath, then went to the cold storage locker and removed the cake saver containing Chrissy's remains. "I promised to return the remains to the old woman that deeply loved this cat," she said, as tears welled up in her eyes. "Can you at least have the decency to return them to me when you're through?"

"I can't guarantee that, but I'll make a note of it in my log," he replied without a hint of compassion.

LeAnn doubted he'd take the time. To avoid breaking down completely, she reverted back to her technical background adding, "You will need to keep that cold if you expect to get any information from the body."

"I have a large cooler in the trunk already iced down. I'm sure that will preserve it properly. Thank you for your assistance. I'll be in touch if we need any additional information."

With that he turned and left. LeAnn felt totally crushed. She knew she and the rest of the Tidal Surge had just lost all the evidence they had.

Chapter 32 - June 5, 2010 – 10:30 AM

L eAnn sat dejectedly in her office blaming herself. She felt she had let down the others. She was emotionally drained and barely had the strength to get up and go home, which was the only thing she could think to do.

As she headed for the door, her clinic phone rang. She thought she'd just let it ring, but changed her mind at the last minute and picked up.

"Roberts Animal Clinic," she uttered anemically. The response from the voice on the phone was a surprise.

"May I speak with LeAnn Roberts? This is Dr. Edwards." His voice jolted LeAnn out of the doldrums.

"Dr. Edwards, what a relief," she replied, suddenly rejuvenated. "I thought you were gone for the weekend."

"Well, I am, but I called into my office to give my assistant some instructions, and he said he had a message from you which sounded pretty urgent."

"Thank you so much for calling me back so promptly. I really need some help. The only person I could think of that would have the expertise I need is you." She then proceeded to describe what had transpired the last few days. After she finished with the results of the necropsy, there was a long moment of silence.

Dr. Edwards finally responded, "You certainly have an intriguing situation. Do you suspect this might be some kind of virus?" he asked.

"I honestly have never seen anything quite like this. I've seen cases of flesh-eating bacteria, but they always had external manifestations. There was no clue anything was wrong until I cut open the cat's abdominal cavity. Besides the lack of internal organs, the fog-like mist that came out was downright menacing."

Again, there was a long silence. Finally, Dr. Edwards acknowledged, "LeAnn, I want to help any way I can. I'll have to see the cat's remains. Can you overnight them to me? Packing them in dry ice would be best."

LeAnn realized she hadn't told him the final chapter. "Dr. Edwards," she said dejectedly, "Homeland Security somehow got my message to our county animal control. Within an hour of me leaving the message, they were here demanding I turn over the cat's remains. They left less than 40 minutes ago. I'm so sorry. But I had to report it for legal and health reasons."

Again, there was a long silence. "LeAnn, I just had a thought. You mentioned that fog being pulled out by the exhaust fan. Does the system have a filtration system?"

"Yes."

"Ok, here's what I want you to do. Very carefully remove those filters. Be sure you have on gloves, some kind of jacket with sleeves closed off, and a mask. In fact, an airpark closed system would do better in protecting your lungs. I have a hunch that whatever this is may be transferred by contact. If there is evidence of anything on the filters, seal them in plastic or preferably glass containers, and overnight them to me. Again, pack them in dry ice. Let me know what you've found."

Dr. Edwards gave her his cell phone number. A ray of hope glimmered in LeAnn's mind. Perhaps not all was lost.

LeAnn located the filtration system manual which identified the location of the filter manifolds. There were two racks of two filters each. Fortunately, the system was designed with maintenance in mind. Marmon clamps secured the outer manifold, inside which were the filters. She removed the clamps and slipped off the manifolds. There was an obvious reddish-brown slime like residue trapped on the filters. It was still moist looking. LeAnn carefully removed each filter and placed them into separate glass containers. When finished, she immediately called Dr. Edwards and gave him the news.

"Ah," sighed Dr. Edwards. "This was what I hoped you'd find. Are these paper or metal sieve type filters?" he asked.

"They look like corrugated paper type elements."

"Does the paper filter material appear like it's being broken down?" questioned Dr. Edwards.

"Yes, in fact it does seem like parts of the filter adjacent to the heaviest concentrations of the 'slime' has been attacked by something."

"That's very troubling," said Dr. Edwards gloomily.

"Why?" asked LeAnn, with a touch of alarm in her voice.

"I don't want to speculate until I've examined this slime you're describing. Please get those filters to me as fast as you can. I just had another thought. Before you send them, get some close-up photos of them, particularly the slime and adjacent filter material. E-mail the photos to me as soon as you take them. Something tells me we don't have time to waste."

LeAnn took pictures and e-mailed them to Dr. Edwards. She then package up the filters, surrounding them in dry ice as instructed. She hand carried the package to Fed Ex, just managing to arrive before they closed. The break-neck pace helped her get past losing Chrissy's remains.

Chapter 33 - June 5, 2010 – 12:30 PM

While LeAnn struggled with phase one of their plan, Quinn and Grace were starting to implement phase two. They arrived at the Seafood at Sundown restaurant right at 12:30. Grace informed the receptionist that they were to meet a Mr. Volker of GG Oil for lunch. She acknowledged immediately and led them efficiently to a table with a wonderful view of the water.

The water was a crystal blue that shimmered in the sunlight as ripples from a gentle sea breeze added a pleasant texture. However, contrary to its tranquil appearance, Quinn and Grace both sensed there was an ominous threat lurking somewhere below the ocean surface, and it was getting closer by the hour.

Two gentlemen were already seated at the table having cocktails. They both rose as Grace and Quinn approached. "I'm Robert Volker" said a portly middle aged balding man about 5'7" tall. "This is Bruce Langstrom, one of our esteemed geologists."

"It's a pleasure to meet you," Langstrom said with a genuine looking smile. "Gee, Bob, you never called me esteemed before," cracked Langstrom. They all laughed at that.

Langstrom was a lanky, tanned man, about forty years old, fitting exactly the image Grace had for a field geologist. Volker was dressed smartly with a sports jacket and tie. Langstrom, however, had on kaki pants and a kaki long sleeve, open-necked shirt giving him that "Indiana Jones" look.

Grace introduced herself and then Quinn. The group all shook hands and sat down at a white, linen-covered round table with fresh flowers as a centerpiece. "This sure is one classy place," Quinn thought to himself. Grace could sense Quinn was getting uncomfortable.

After ordering a round of drinks and exchanging business cards, which Quinn had forgot to bring, Volker opened the conversation by asking, "Grace, you are a reporter for the Gulf Coast Times, correct?"

"That's right," she answered with an inviting smile. Her looks were not lost on Volker. "By the way," she added, "do you mind if I record our conversations? I'm not particularly good at taking notes and I have a feeling this might get somewhat technical."

"That's ok by me," Volker replied. "Are you ok with that, Bruce?"

Langstrom nodded yes with a smile. Grace flipped on the recorder.

"As I mentioned to you on the phone," Grace continued, "Quinton and I are trying to work up a report on the history of oil and how geology is used to identify oil-bearing formations. Quinton is an amateur archeologist and wants to tie in the type of organisms that might have been the building blocks of the oil in the first place." Grace nodded toward Quinn as she spoke.

Quinn added, "My main interest is in the Paleozoic Era, and of particular interest is the Permian Period. As I'm sure Mr. Langstrom knows, the Permian Period ended with the largest mass extinction of life in Earth's history. I thought perhaps since GG has extracted oil from some of the deepest wells ever drilled that you might have some enlightening information."

Volker seemed to ponder that idea for a moment.

Wanting to put a soft spin on things, Grace said, "If we can show

how cooperative GG Oil is in wanting to enhance education, I think it would help show your positive influence in the community."

With that Volker smiled and retorted, "Grace, are you sure you're not more than a reporter? You'd make a mighty good sales executive." They all smiled.

"Bruce," Volker said, "do you have any information for Grace and Quinton?"

Langstrom looked relaxed and answered with a smile, "You are correct, Quinton. The Permian Period is the last period of the Paleozoic Era, and there was a mass extinction prior to the start of the next geological period called the Mesozoic Era. The Mesozoic became known as the age of the dinosaurs.

There are numerous theories of what caused the mass extinction prior to the dinosaur age. Some believe in a meteorite impact, other theories suggest extensive volcanic eruptions, still others suspect a massive release of methane gas trapped in water molecules. I personally believe the oceans became severely deficient in oxygen toward the end of the Permian Period. This caused sulfate-reducing bacteria to become a dominate force in the oceans, resulting in vast emissions of hydrogen sulfide which poisoned plant and animal life on both land and sea. The hydrogen sulfide would also have weakened the ozone layer, exposing much of the life that remained to fatal levels of UV radiation."

"Wow, this is getting a bit technical for me. Quinn, any comments?" Grace asked.

Quinn jumped in, "I know each of the theories you mentioned has some supporting evidence, but also refuting evidence as well. Have you found anything in your core samples from the deep water well that supports the deficient oxygen levels in the ocean theory? Any idea on what might have caused the oxygen levels to decrease?"

Volker looked like he was getting nervous when the deepwater well was mentioned. However, he let Langstrom continue.

"There are many questions that are unanswered. We're confident there was a spike upward in oxygen and a corresponding drop in carbon dioxide in the Mississippian Epoch which was before the Permian, about 310 million years ago. We don't know why that occurred either. The core samples we got during our Deep Water Horizon drilling suggest that as we approached the oil-bearing rock, which based on accepted dating techniques, was from the Permian Period, there was a significant reduction in species that had carbonate hard parts, like shells. This would support the theory of excessive carbon dioxide levels in the ocean."

Grace with a sincere look asked, "What about the oil leaking into the ocean? Does that show anything different from other crude oil? I'm assuming you routinely take samples of crude oil that comes from wells, right?"

"We certainly do," answered Langstrom. "I'm not a chemist, but I understand that umm… there wasn't any significant difference in this oil." Langstrom stiffened slightly and seemed to be choosing his words more carefully.

Grace, trying to politely dig deeper, continued, "I know there has been concern about the dispersants used to help break down the crude oil. Have you used various kinds and do you check samples for oil breakdown effects?"

Langstrom answered, "Of course we check samples before and after addition of the dispersants. And we have tried various types. The most recent one called …"

Volker interrupted Langstrom at that point. "It seems like we're straying from our agreed-upon topic of discussion," he said more emphatically than he intended. "There are things we consider proprietary, and would prefer not to make public until we have management approval. I'm sure you understand, Grace."

"I understand completely," she said, although her disappointment was obvious.

The conversation continued amiably for the rest of the meal, which was more than equal to the restaurant's excellent reputation. However, on several occasions Volker directed the topics toward more general information. Grace and Quinn were very impressed by Langstrom, both by his knowledge and his attempts to be as honest as possible.

One of the last things Grace questioned was, "Getting back to the crude oil samples, do you have a … let's say, an expert chemist that you rely on for testing crucial samples related to the oil spill? Could we possibly speak to him maybe via a conference call if he's at a distant location? Mr. Volker, you could act as a moderator if you'd prefer."

Langstrom glanced questioningly at Volker who appeared to be very uncomfortable with the question. "Yes, we do have what we call Technical Fellows who are chosen for their experience and expertise, and are at the highest pay level attainable in the company on the technical path rather than the executive path. We did have a technical fellow heading up the oil spill sample analysis, but he is not …ah…. not presently available. Langstrom looked down at his plate with a disapproving gaze, and seemed to lose his relaxed air of confidence.

With that, Volker signaled for the check and said, "We really must get back to work. I do hope we were able to provide you useful information and your article will be favorable toward GG. Please let me know when it will be appearing in your paper as I certainly am interested in what your conclusions will be."

Grace responded pleasantly, "We truly appreciate the time you've taken out of your hectic schedules."

Quinn added, "Thank you so much for the wealth of information you've provided today and the candor in your answers."

They all stood and shook hands.

As they waited for their cars from the valet, Quinn spoke with Langstrom mentioning he'd like to get together sometime to talk "shop". "Maybe you could talk at one of our amateur archeologist meetings at the junior college," he offered.

Langstrom seemed genuinely interested and said, "You've got my card. Give me a call."

Volker's car arrived first and he said his goodbyes and drove off. The three stood there waiting for their cars, and Langstrom looked nervous for the first time. Finally, he said apologetically, "I'm sorry if I couldn't answer all your questions as completely as I would have liked. You have my card. Perhaps we could talk another time off the record." He looked toward the ground and added, "There are things I'm not particularly happy about."

Grace could see Langstrom was struggling with something and answered, "What are you referring to Bruce?"

"It concerns the way things have been handled relative to the oil spill," he replied, but let's talk another time after hours." His car arrived. He shook both their hands, then drove off.

Grace was nearly overcome with excitement. "I think we just witnessed a breakthrough" she cheered.

"We better get together with him soon before he has second thoughts." said Quinn.

Grace added, "Yeah, knowing corporate mantras, I'll bet he could lose his job in an instant if he violates policy, even if it's the ethical thing to do."

. As they drove home they decided maybe it would be best for Quinn to call and meet with Langstrom. That way Langstrom wouldn't be intimidated by the presence of a representative of the news media.

*****

By now it was 2:30 PM and Quinn suggested calling LeAnn to find out how she made out with phase one and fill her in on their progress. Putting his cell phone on speaker so Grace could hear he dialed up LeAnn.

LeAnn answered seeming nearly out of breath, "Quinn your timing is unbelievable. I'm just leaving Fed-Ex. I had to run before they closed the door."

"Why, what's happening?"

LeAnn answered hesitantly, "I've good news and bad news. I contacted Dr. Edwards and he's anxious to help us. I just finished sending him the filters from the clinic's exhaust system because they definitely had residue on them. That's the good news."

"Why not send him Chrissy's remains so he can see them first hand?" Quinn asked.

"That's the bad news. I called into the County Animal Control thinking we'd be clear until Monday morning. Within an hour I got a call from a guy named Barlow from Homeland Security. He was already at my place and took Chrissy's remains as soon as I got there. Quinn, I'm sorry."

There was silence for a moment, but LeAnn was sure Quinn was fuming. Finally, Quinn cussed, "God Damn it. I'm not mad at you, LeAnn. I'm just mad. Homeland Security again. They seem to be one step ahead of us at every turn. Plus, they never give us a straight answer."

Grace added, "LeAnn, you did the best you could."

"Thanks. Dr. Edwards did feel he could get something from the filter residue, so maybe there's still hope." None of them were really convinced.

Grace and Quinn then summarized the meeting they'd had with GG Oil for LeAnn. Quinn finished by saying, "I'm going to try to speak with Langstrom tonight. Both Grace and I feel like we have a potential ally in Langstrom. Depending on how the conversation goes, I'd be willing to tell him most of what we know. Any objections?"

LeAnn and Grace both agreed. LeAnn added, "I think we should get all of us together again maybe Sunday evening so everyone knows the latest. That way Luther and Jesse have as much as possible to hit the politicians with on Monday."

"Great idea," acknowledged Quinn.

Chapter 34 - June 5, 2010 – 6:00 PM

B y 6:00 PM that evening Quinn couldn't wait any longer. He had dropped off Grace at her house around 3:30 then went home himself to rest or so he hoped. But once again he was wound up too tight to relax. He wanted to call Langstrom right away but didn't want to seem too anxious. So he waited, but now had reached the end of his rope.

Langstrom's business card had his office phone and his cell phone, so Quinn tried his cell. Langstrom answered with a hearty "Hello."

"Bruce, this is Quinn Jones. I hope I'm not interrupting your dinner."

"No, not at all," replied Langstrom. "After that huge lunch, I was thinking I'd skip dinner altogether. The wife's away visiting her mother in Birmingham, so I'm kind of doing the bachelor thing this weekend."

Quinn laughed, "You know I'm a confirmed bachelor myself, so I know the feeling. Hey, how about having a beer and shooting some pool tonight? You interested?"

"That sounds better than what I'm doing, which is absolutely nothing."

"Do you know Tommy's Tavern? They have a nice selection of draft beers and four new pool tables. How about 7:30?"

"Sounds like a winner," answered Langstrom. "See you there."

They both arrived at about the same time. Langstrom tried a local brew called Bayou Beast while Quinn stuck with Guinness. They got along great and by 9:00 PM they were tied at two racks apiece and on their third round of drafts. Quinn was not a heavy drinker and decided he better get to the point before he forgot what the point was. He said to Langstrom, "How about taking a break at one of those booths and ordering a burger?"

"Yeah, I am finally getting a little hungry," Langstrom said. "I think you're really trying to break my rhythm though since I put the hurt on you the last two games."

"Never entered my mind," Quinn replied, grinning.

After ordering burgers and some fries, Quinn continued the conversation, "Bruce I have to admit something to you. Grace and I were not completely upfront with you and Volker at lunch today. I mean, we are who we said we were as far as our jobs and interests. However, writing that newspaper article was not our top priority." Langstrom's look changed to a suspicious gaze.

"I'm going to be totally honest with you now because I believe you're honest and basically a guy that wants to do the right thing." Langstrom's gaze softened a bit. Quinn told him most of what had occurred over the last few days. He mentioned the cat autopsy but didn't mention the fog, the filters and residue, or that they had Dr. Edwards involved. He didn't mention Luther or Jesse either.

The more Quinn described what had happened, the more interested and concerned Langstrom became. Quinn finished his description then asked, "Earlier today you mentioned you were disturbed about what was happening and perhaps that some of the information on the crude oil leak was being withheld. Could you possibly elaborate?"

Langstrom hesitated and Quinn thought he might have pushed too hard. But Langstrom finally spoke, "Volker mentioned that we had our expert, or "Fellow" as our company identifies them, working the crude oil samples from the Gulf leak. That part was true. But he said our "Fellow" wasn't available for a meeting with you. The reason he's not available is because he's dead." Quinn's breath caught in his throat at that comment.

Langstrom went on, "His name was Werner Strauss and without a doubt he was the best organic chemist we had. I didn't know him real well, but he had given a presentation at one of our workshops. The guy deserved the title of "Fellow" more than anyone I've met."

Quinn was riveted on every word. "What happened to him?" whispered Quinn trying to get his voice under control.

"He died of an apparent heart attack," answered Langstrom. "That's the company's official position and Werner did have a history of at least two previous heart attacks. However, the strange thing is his body was removed and buried very quickly, and there was never an announcement on a funeral. Quite a few people asked about it because he was well liked within the company. Management had no comment. In addition, the rumor is he was evaluating samples of crude oil from the leak when he died. Supposedly he was mixing them with that new dispersal agent I started to mention when Volker cut me off. I doubt whether that had anything to do with his death, but it adds fuel to the fire."

Quinn had so many questions he didn't know where to start. "How long ago was this?" questioned Quinn.

"Well, it was the middle of May, around the 12th, I think."

"Was this Werner working by himself?"

Langstrom seemed to be getting jittery, but answered, "Werner was on night shift because of his health, kind of light duty so to speak. There was a new guy with him, but I honestly don't know his name. Come to think of it, the guy kind of disappeared from the radar. I hadn't really thought about that until you asked."

"Bruce, I'm really sorry to keep bugging you about this," Quinn said apologetically. "I know you're going out on a limb just talking to me. But I have a feeling you're as concerned about what's going on here as I am. No one in authority is offering any real answers. There have been deaths on a wide scale at least in the ocean, and maybe four and now five humans. Why all the secrecy? What really worries me is maybe this is just the tip of the iceberg."

Langstrom nodded, his face showing the stress.

"Bruce, could this new dispersal agent be a key? Do you know anything else about it?"

"All I really know is it is proprietary. Rumor is it came from the military. I'm not even sure if it was used on any of the crude oil plumes."

"Who might know that?"

"It would probably be someone from our crude oil containment division. I'm not really sure who that would be, but I'll try to find out for you. Come to think of it, usually in a situation like the Deep Horizon explosion, our company sets up a disaster response team. They make all the decisions on how the entire investigation is to be run. This disaster seems to be more compartmentalized with one team not knowing what other teams are doing. Decisions seem to be made at a very high level without always consulting the working team managers. Maybe that's because of the enormous costs involved."

Quinn sighed, "Seems like doing the right thing should be the primary driver not cost. Well, I know there are a lot more questions I should be asking, but I'm about stressed out. Do you want to play a winner takes all rack?"

"To be honest with you, I think I'm done for the night. That Bayou Beast must be about 10% alcohol because I'm suddenly feeling it."

"Listen," Quinn said. "I truly appreciate you talking about this, and shooting pool. We'll have to do this again without the interrogation."

"Yeah," Langstrom said, "I enjoyed the pool and conversation to. If I hear anything more, I'll keep in touch. I'd really like to hear what you find out."

"I'll keep you informed," Quinn said. They shook hands and headed their separate ways.

Chapter 35 - June 6, 2010 – 8:00 PM

T he Tidal Surge Group met briefly to summarize what they found. Even Dr. Edwards called in, mostly to listen since he wouldn't receive the filter samples until Monday morning.

LeAnn spoke on her unfortunate run-in with Homeland Security and having to turn over Chrissy's remains. Grace discussed their conversation with Volker and Langstrom, and Quinn filled everyone in on his Saturday evening meeting with Langstrom.

Luther and Jesse touched on what they planned to ask Senator Lee. Luther also said he had contacts with the people that cleaned the GG Oil labs. He thought perhaps they picked up on what might have happened. As Luther put it, "Often times people don't pay attention to the cleaning crews or what they throw in the trash." Luther also said they'd try to find out more on the person that was helping Werner Strauss when he died.

Jesse mentioned, "It sure would be helpful if Langstrom can come up with a name."

Dr. Edwards concluded the meeting indicating he would get right on the residue analysis as soon as the filters arrived. He felt he could have preliminary results by Tuesday evening and suggested a meeting at 8:00 PM EST to update the group. They all agreed.

Chapter 36 - June 7, 2010 – 9:00 AM

Luther and Jesse arrived at the Baton Rouge State Capitol at 9:00 AM. Their meeting with Senator Lee was at 9:30, but they wanted plenty of time to get through security and still have some time to review their plans. Per Luther's suggestion, Jesse would portray himself as Luther's assistant mostly involved with security. Although Luther's original meeting objective was funding, he now felt the emphasis needed to be on information about Homeland Security's involvement in the oil spill, and the mystery of the missing four bodies. He still was struggling with how to get those items on the agenda.

At 9:30 AM sharp an aid to Senator Lee, named Charles Adams, announced that the Senator would see them now. They were ushered into a plush office with a huge mahogany desk. From behind, the desk was framed by bookshelves filled neatly with law books. A large picture of Senator Lee shaking hands with President Obama adorned the wall between the bookshelves. The United States Flag and the Louisiana State Flag stood to the senators left, and a tray with coffee and tea in sterling decanters and a sterling plate of Danish was laid out on a matching mahogany end table to the right. A small plush dark leather couch with two matching leather chairs faced the desk.

The aid introduced Luther and Jesse. Senator Lee rose and extended his hand and said with a machine-like smile and deep southern drawl, "Gentlemen, it is a pleasure to meet you. Please be seated." He motioned for them to choose the leather couch.

Senator Lee continued, "Mr. Brown, I understand you have undertaken a plan to fill a definite need in our community to help the homeless and disadvantaged. The State certainly supports helping those who need it most."

"Thank you Senator," replied Luther. "I'm hoping you will reinforce your support with some financial sustenance as well."

"Ah, Mr. Brown," smiled Senator Lee, "I'd heard you like to get right to the point."

Luther returned the smile and added, "Well, I'd hate to impose extra strain on your busy schedule with idle chatter. I was hoping the state might contribute at least 50% of the cost to refurbish the mission and initiate an advertisement campaign to raise the remaining 50% through donations. Of course, I'll be asking for donations throughout my other missions, which by the way, have been self-sustaining by the second year of operation. We train our people to contribute back to the community by offering various service type jobs. We've had excellent reports from individuals and companies that have hired our workers. It's really a win/win situation for all concerned."

"I have already purchased an old building," continued Luther, "about half way between here and the coast. It is useable, but in dire need of renovation. I have about thirty homeless people living there already. I try to do background checks on them to make sure there are no outstanding warrants for their arrests, but that's difficult to establish. Perhaps someone from Homeland Security could assist with those checks through some kind of computerized database."

"I am impressed," returned Senator Lee. "You may be in luck as the southern regional director of Homeland Security, Director James Simmons, is in fact here. We had a brief meeting earlier this morning."

Senator Lee motioned to his aid who had been listening to the discussion in one of the side chairs, "Charles, please see if you can locate Director Simmons and have him join us." Charles nodded and exited quietly through a side door.

Senator Lee continued, "Mr. Brown, I'll discuss with our budget director whether we have any discretionary funds we could tap into. As you know, with economic times as they are, our budget is stretched awfully thin. If we can find anything at all, it would be very limited, perhaps $50,000 at the most."

Luther replied, "Senator Lee, that would go a long way toward at least getting plumbing and electrical services updated."

With that, the side door opened and Charles and Director Simmons entered. Senator Lee said, "Thank you Charles," then made the introductions. They continued with discussing the possibility of utilizing existing data bases to track criminals and potential illegal aliens.

On cue from Luther, Jesse weighed into the conversation by acknowledging, "Director Simmons, the data bases you've mentioned will be very helpful. However, I'm curious about something. From all the news reports, I know Homeland Security has been involved in the Deepwater Horizon investigation. How did Homeland Security get involved in the first place? Was there concern about terrorist sabotage?"

Simmons seemed surprised at the question, glancing at Senator Lee before answering. "Well," he said clearing his throat, "actually both Senator Lee and myself were asked to become involved to show solidarity and responsibility from both the State of Louisiana and the nation."

Jesse looked confused by the answer, which was intentionally vague. Jesse was about to question who asked them to get involved when Luther jumped in, "There has been a lot of talk at the mission about deaths near the oil spill and concern that jobs and maybe more lives are at stake. Homeless folk are at more risk than most when environmental catastrophes occur because they don't have any shelter to protect them. They get very nervous when natural disasters happen."

Senator Lee, who was getting apprehensive with the line of questioning, answered, "I'm not aware of any deaths."

Director Simmons interrupted, "Where did you hear about this? Surely you don't consider street people rumors reliable." Simmons immediately knew he said the wrong thing.

Luther responded calmly, "You would be surprised at the resourcefulness of many of the disadvantaged. In fact, I heard the specific quantity of deaths was four."

Director Simmons eyes hardened and a shadow of irritation passed over Senator Lee's face. "I didn't mean any disrespect for the people you represent, Mr. Brown," Simmons warned, "but I'd suggest you be cautious about divulging that type of information without substantiating it first."

"You're correct," Luther replied. "I was just trying to ease their fears if you knew something to the contrary." Luther's response hung in the air like a bad odor.

Finally Senator Lee announced both he and Simmons had another meeting scheduled and needed to bring this meeting to an end. They all shook hands and Luther thanked them for the opportunity to discuss funding with them. Senator Lee reiterated that he would discuss funding with his budget advisor and have one of his aids get in touch with Luther.

"Where is the best place to contact you, Mr. Brown?" queried Senator Lee.

"I'll be spending most of my time for the rest of this week at the mission," Luther replied. "You can always reach me at my cell phone number." He handed Senator Lee and Director Simmons his business card, commenting that the address of the mission was on the card as well as his phone number. With that they were escorted from the office by Charles.

As the door closed Senator Lee growled, "Simmons, what the hell is this about, four bodies? I knew about the chemist at GG Oil, but I never heard about anyone else. Are they related?"

"We don't think so," Simmons answered. "We think it was some kind of drug deal gone bad. Since the urgency wasn't there, we haven't really investigated the cause of death yet."

Lee replied, "I don't want any turds on my doorstep. I think you better verify cause of death right quick, and get someone down to that mission. I don't like the way this is headed. Maybe you can find something there and shut the place down before it ever gets off the ground. These people seem to know more than they're telling."

"I'll take care of it," Simmons answered, "and don't get so paranoid."

*****

After they left the capital, Jesse asked Luther, "What just happened in there?"

"I think we got at least part of our answer," replied Luther. "Both Senator Lee and Homeland Security were brought into this by someone. But if it was someone of national prominence, I suspect name dropping would have happened. If it was the president or a cabinet member, we would have been told. This implies to me that it's more localized."

"But who would have that kind of clout?" Jesse asked with a quizzical frown.

"I wish I knew, but we're sure going to try to find out," replied Luther. "Secondly," added Luther, "I think we hit a raw nerve on the four deaths. Simmons got real defensive when I mentioned the number, so I think a body count of four is correct. My bet is he has the bodies somewhere and Lee is in on this as well."

"You know we're up against some big guns." quipped Jesse. "I sure hope David can beat Goliath at least one more time."

Chapter 37 - June 8, 2010 – 8:00 PM

The Tidal Surge Group met in Grace's office. They were all tensely awaiting Dr. Edward's call. It finally came at 8:30 PM. Grace answered the phone and said, "Dr. Edwards, we're all here and anxiously awaiting your results. Hopefully you have some good news and probably some bad." The positive mood didn't last long.

"Well, not really," answered Dr. Edwards. "I have bad news and I'm afraid worse news. But first let me give you a theory I've developed." The group looked expectantly at one another.

Dr. Edwards continued, "We've established, based on Langstrom's input, that this oil came from the geological time period called the Permian. We've never encountered crude oil from this era. We also know that there was an increase in atmospheric oxygen levels prior to the Permian period, although the cause of that we don't know. Finally, and most disturbing, is that the largest mass extinction of life in Earth's history occurred at the end of the Permian period. The cause of that we don't know conclusively either."

All eyes were riveted on the telephone as if it held the answer. "Let's suppose, continued Dr. Edwards, "that there was some virus, bacteria, or other microbe, source unknown, that was the actual cause of the extinction. It became trapped in the crude oil molecules formed by the dying life it destroyed. It's been dormant ever since. The microbes remain dormant unless there is an increase in the levels of oxygen above our present day levels, perhaps similar to what occurred before the Permian Period. I believe the oxygen levels are the key to unleashing this "plague", but I'm struggling with how that might happen."

Grace was the first to respond. "Dr. Edwards, you said plague. Do you have a concern that we actually might have released something?"

"That's the worse news," answered Dr. Edwards. "The filter residue from the fog emanating from Chrissy's body was full of what I think was a reproductive form of the microbe. Worse yet, it is a crossover type pathogen and extremely virulent."

"What do you mean by crossover?" asked Quinn.

"It means it not only attacks one species," replied Dr. Edwards. "It affects many. I'm still running tests, but I fear it may impact plants as well as fish and mammals. I'm not sure of insects and reptiles, but the mass extinction encompassed all life forms. In essence, if this gets unleashed and we're unable to contain it, it could be the death of life as we know it."

There was dead silence as the group tried to grasp what had been just presented. Finally, Dr. Edwards spoke again, "I expect the extinction in the past took perhaps hundreds of thousands of years to run its course. I believe that because it appears the microbes are spread by direct contact. In the case of sea life, the dying would sink to the bottom of the ocean, come in contact with bottom dwelling life, and continue the die off. Ocean currents would spread things slowly. Fish and other life forms might spread it faster, particularly if they were of a migratory nature. On land, wind currents would transfer the fog clouds from dying animals. Carnivorous animals and scavengers would also spread the virus. Wind currents would move leaves and seed pods from plants to adjacent plants, and herbivores would also become infected. Insects might be carriers also pollinating plants with the disease before dying themselves."

"As I mentioned, the microbes are extremely infective. Incidental contact seems to be sufficient to cause death. I've tried it on laboratory mice and both salt water and fresh water fish. In every case it was fatal, with death occurring within one to three hours. I've done two autopsies on infected mice. Destruction of internal organs was similar to what LeAnn reported in the cat. For mammals it appears to attack the lungs first where oxygen transfer to the blood occurs. There are multiple questions that need to be answered, especially what species are impacted and whether lethality changes as the virus is passed onto the next host. Most importantly, I haven't begun to consider how to neutralize this thing. I need help, and it better be soon or we could be on the threshold of another mass extinction."

Dr. Edwards concluded by saying, "I guess in today's environment with mass transportation of people and produce, if this really is what I think it might be, extinctions could happen faster, much faster than in the past."

"What do we do now?" questioned Quinn finally. "I wouldn't want to be the one to yell fire in the packed theater until we know for sure."

"I agree," said Luther, "but the longer we wait to cry wolf, the harder it could be to contain the problem. Dr. Edwards, do you know what stops this bug?"

"Not yet," replied Dr. Edwards. "I'm just now trying to get a rough idea of what species might be impacted. I can tell you this. We need a lot of investigative help before we get our arms around this. In fact, we need worldwide help."

LeAnn finally spoke up. "Would it be of any value to check the reefs in the area of the fish kill to see if they have been impacted?"

"That's an excellent idea," responded Dr. Edwards. "That would also tell us how fast this thing is progressing."

"I've got a boat," said Quinn. "All we need are some experienced divers."

Grace added, "If the reef shows signs of stress, I think we should blow the lid off this immediately. We'd better get video proof for documentation though."

"One more thing," mentioned Dr. Edwards. "Can we find out what happened to the four bodies that were briefly at Ginger's hospital, and that Werner Strauss fellow? We really need to know how they died and what exposure, if any, they had to the crude oil."

All eyes looked to Luther. "I asked my cleaning contacts that work at the GG Oil Labs, but I haven't got any feedback yet. I'll bug them again and let them know it's urgent."

The group's mood was somber. Quinn finally responded, "This has to get elevated fast. The question is do we wait until we have more proof or sound the alarm now."

Grace answered, "My deadline to my editor is tomorrow to give him a reason why I should be spending full time on this. He's a street savvy guy and a great sounding board. I think I should present what we have and get his opinion. Meanwhile, perhaps Luther and Jesse can find out more on Werner Strauss's death, who his co-worker was, and what happened to the other bodies. Quinn, I'd like you to join me tomorrow. I think you and my editor will relate well to one another."

"Ok," Quinn said. "Let's get moving. I fear we'll need good luck and divine intervention to pull this off." Everyone realized that statement was one of the few things they knew for sure.

Chapter 38 - June 9, 2010 – 8:10 AM

Wednesday morning dawned as another steamy southern day. Quinn felt anything but hot. He and the other members of the Tidal Surge did not seem to be any closer to learning what, why, how, or even if any of the deaths had anything to do with the crude oil leak.

As Quinn was getting ready to meet with Grace to review how to present what they'd learned to Grace's editor, his phone rang. The voice on the other end said, "Quinn, this is Bruce Langstrom."

Quinn, with a surprised voice, answered, "Hey, Bruce, how are you?"

"Listen," said Langstrom, "I was able to get some information for you on names of people at GG Oil to help answer some of your questions from the other night. Thought I'd pass it on. Ronald Strong is the department manager for chemical analysis. Werner Strauss, the Fellows Chemist that died, worked for him. Strong would also have to have approved use of the dispersant before it was sprayed. He should know whether it was actually used."

"Secondly, the guy that was working in the lab with Strauss when he died was Timothy Gardner. He's a new guy only out of college a few months. But if you're thinking of contacting him, forget it. I found out he was sent on a field assignment a couple days after Strauss's death."

Quinn, trying to grasp the scope of this revelation asked, "Do you know where he was sent to?"

Langstrom replied with a sarcastic tone, "Siberia, can you believe it? We sent a small team of five people to work with Gasprom, the Russian oil and gas giant. They're exploring some potential oil fields in Siberia, and GG Oil wants to partner with them if possible. I can tell you this. Asking why Gardner was chosen hit a lot of raw nerves. You can draw your own conclusions."

"Quinn, I've got to go. Good luck with your investigation."

Quinn added, "Bruce, I can't tell you how much this helps. Thanks so much. I'll let you know what we find out." They both hung up.

Quinn quickly dialed up Luther to give him and Jesse the information. After getting the information, Luther replied, "I got confirmation from my cleaning contact that Tim Gardner was in fact the guy working with Strauss when he died. I also found out Gardner was quite the lady's man and made a lot of calls that night. I'm going to have Jesse search his cell phone call record for that night, which was May 12, 2010. There may be some good leads there."

"Is that legal?" asked Quinn hesitantly.

"Well, not exactly," replied Luther. "But I think we're at a point where we've got to go after this aggressively."

Luther continued, "Apparently the May 12th night shift was full of action at the lab. A rush job of crude oil samples mixed with some new dispersant came in right near shift change which was why Strauss got involved. However, the emergency folks didn't show up until after 11:00 PM. Putting two and two together, it seems like Strauss and Gardner must have worked most of the night on the analysis.

However, per the cleaning folks, Strauss was old-school; always hand writing reports before having someone else put them into the computer in the final version. The cleaning folks always had a wastepaper basket full of scratch paper notes and report drafts. Interestingly, there was nothing that night, and it didn't appear GG's internal security removed anything. Something is strange about that, but I just can't put my finger on it."

Luther added, "Jesse seems to be a natural private investigator. He doesn't mind fabricating stories to get information. In addition to following up on the cell phone leads, I'll have Jesse contact that Ron Strong."

"Also, I'd suggest you and Grace push her editor pretty hard for direction on how to approach alerting the nation and maybe the entire world. We need big time help to find out how to stop this virus, or whatever it is, from starting another mass extinction."

"So you really believe that's what we're facing?" asked Quinn.

"Yes, I do," responded Luther. "To tell you the truth, I'm scared."

Quinn stated, "I'll plan on meeting you at your mission after Grace and I meet with her editor. I suspect it'll be early afternoon."

"Sounds good," replied Luther. "Let's get to it."

Chapter 39 - June 9, 2010 – 11:45 AM

L uther had given Jesse the information from Quinn and Langstrom and told Jesse to use every means he could think of to get the answers they needed. Jesse was happy to finally be contributing. Luther had put him onto a computer hacker named Earl who was as close to a genius as he'd ever seen. For a hundred dollars, two six packs, and a promise to include him in the story if any book was written on this "adventure", as he put it, Earl hacked into the phone system data base and extracted Tim Gardner's calls for a week before and a week after May 12th. Earl also pulled up who the cell phones were registered to.

Reviewing the printouts, Jesse noted most of the calls were to the same five female names. However, on the morning of May 12th and again about 5:00 PM, Gardner made two calls to a phone registered to an Anthony Feretta. Jesse had a hunch and asked Earl if he could find out anything about the Feretta family. "No problem," scoffed Earl, and with a few clicks of his mouse had the entire Feretta family bios, which included a son age 12, and a 16-year-old daughter named Tina.

"Well, well," smiled Jesse. "Maybe good ole' Timmy had more than one reason to go to Siberia, as in avoiding a statutory rape charge or being shot by Tina's old man. I think a personal call to Tina might be quite revealing."

He figured Tina would be in high school and might have an

early lunch schedule. With kids of his own, Jesse knew they loved to text and talk on the phone over lunch, so he gave Tina's cell a call. Per Luther's recommendation, Jesse had made a cash purchase of a throwaway cell phone so his calls couldn't be traced.

It was his lucky day as a soft, almost innocent voice answered, "Hello."

Jesse, in the most authoritative voice he could muster, said, "Is this Tina Feretta?"

"Yes, who is this?" responded Tina with a lyrical humorous voice. "I can tell it's you Franky."

"I'm sorry miss, this isn't Franky. My name is Lt. Charles Romex with the FBI," lied Jesse.

"FBI," shrieked Tina. "Am I in some sort of trouble?" her voice now shaking noticeably.

Jesse decided to take a chance that his haunch was right. "That all depends on you," replied Jesse. "If you cooperate with me, I think I can keep this between us and not get your parents involved."

"Ok, ok. Please, just don't tell my Dad," lamented Tina. Jesse began to think Tina had more than one problem to worry about.

"Are you where we can talk privately?" asked Jesse.

"Let me go outside," said Tina. Jesse could hear conversations in the background and then a door open then shut with a thud. "Ok, I'm alone," said Tina.

"Do you know a Tim Gardner?" asked Jesse.

"Huh?" said Tina obviously totally surprised by the question.

"I know you had several phone conversations with him on May 12th," Jesse added with a much harsher tone.

"Yes, I know him," replied Tina sheepishly, "but I only talked to him on the phone."

"Let's get something straight, Tina. I won't press any charges for your other activities if you give me straight answers about Gardner," Jesse emphasized, hoping she wasn't exactly a model citizen.

"All right," said Tina. "I did go out with him on one date, but haven't heard from him since. We had pizza that night about 6:00 PM and then I went to his apartment until about 11:00. I remember he said he had to get back to work before second shift was over."

Jesse's heart was pounding. "You mean you spent the entire evening from 6:00 to 11:00 PM with him on May 12th?" Jesse asked.

"That's right. Is he wanted or something? I thought he was cute."

Jesse replied with a hard nose voice, "You don't need to be concerned about him. I do appreciate the information. However, I request you keep our conversation to yourself. As long as no one else knows, your parents won't find out either. If I need anything else, I'll be in touch." With that he hung up.

Chapter 40 - June 9, 2010 – 1:00 PM

J esse felt he was on a roll, so he decided to try a similar routine with Ron Strong from GG Oil. Jesse was learning if he offered just enough data to sound credible, he usually could get the information he needed. Jesse had to go through the company operator because he didn't have Strong's company phone number. He told the operator he was Charles Odem from the EPA.

In a few moments Strong came on the line. "Hello, this is Ron Strong," answered Strong.

"Good morning Mr. Strong. This is Charles Odem from the EPA," lied Jesse. He was getting better at it by the minute.

Strong responded, "Do you work for Jason Lovell? He said he'd be getting back to me."

Jesse had to think fast. "Well, no" Jesse said. "We're in different departments actually. I apologize. Our left and right hands don't always know what each other are doing. I'm calling about the dispersants sprayed on the crude oil plumes from the Deep Horizon oil leak. He wasn't discussing that with you, was he?"

"No, different subject." replied Strong. "It would be good if the EPA designated one person to coordinate contacts with us so I don't have to answer questions from multiple people," added Strong with an irritated tone in his voice.

Jesse knew he better not piss off this guy, so he decided to get to the point quickly. "I am sorry." said Jesse. "We'll get with our managers to set up a point of contact to coordinate all calls with you." Jesse again played a hunch that back in May, GG Oil was anxious to try almost anything to minimize financial risk, and that they sprayed the dispersant the next day after the samples were analyzed by Werner Strauss. "I just have one question really. Was the new dispersant sprayed on May 13th approved based on chemical analysis?"

There was a distinct hesitation by Strong. He finally replied, "All our dispersants are thoroughly evaluated before they are used."

"But you did spray it, correct?" asked Jesse.

"Yes, but application was limited to the Logan plume only," answered Strong.

Jesse followed up cautiously, "I understand this was different from other dispersants used previously. Can you give me the type of dispersant and chemical composition so I can review it?"

Again, there was a long pause. Then Strong answered abruptly, "This is considered proprietary. I suggest you set up a meeting with our legal counsel and forward a detailed list of what information you want prior to the meeting."

Jesse was taken aback by the sudden coldness of the response, and decided further questions would only make things worse. Jesse replied, "Ok. I'll set that meeting up, Mr. Strong. Thank you for your help. We will try to minimize the number of people contacting you." With that he said goodbye and hung up.

Jesse felt this "Private I" gig wasn't half bad. He had found out two important things. First, Gardner wasn't even at the lab during the dispersant analysis. Second, GG Oil did spray the new dispersant on May 13th and only on the Logan plume. Not bad for about an hour's work. He called Luther and gave him an update.

Chapter 41 - June 9, 2010 – 11:30 AM

While Jesse was doing his private investigator imitation, Quinn and Grace had a 10:30AM meeting with Grace's editor, Leon. When they entered his office, Leon sensed the urgency by the stress on their faces. Grace introduced Quinn. "It's a pleasure to meet you, Quinn." said Leon cheerfully. "You two look like you're carrying the world's problems on your shoulders."

"I think we are," Grace said without a hint of humor. Leon's office door was almost always open, but this time he got up from his desk and shut it behind them.

"Ok. What's the scoop?" asked Leon. Grace proceeded to summarize what they'd been through the past week. Leon stopped her several times with questions. Quinn filled in the parts about Homeland Security and LeAnn's autopsy of Chrissy.

Grace finished with, "Leon, we came to you for advice on what to do next. We have to go public with this before it's too late."

Leon could feel the tension in the room. "Ok. Let me get this straight. You have no proof of human deaths. We have an eyewitness of the condition of the cat but have no actual remains to verify that story. There was a large fish kill but no remains from that either. We suspect a new oil dispersant was used somewhere but don't know that for sure. And we have a maverick researcher with a theory that the crude oil spill might have released some type of plague. Have I missed any of the pertinent points?"

Quinn added sheepishly, "We think Homeland Security and GG Oil are covering this up."

"Right, right," said Leon sarcastically.

Both Grace and Quinn looked at the floor knowing that when viewed from a high level, their story was really weak. Leon finally spoke again, "Look, this seems like one hell of a story, almost like a sci-fi thriller. But I can't release this without more substantiation. I'd be crucified if there was another explanation. I tell you what, let's order in some lunch and we can discuss this as we eat. I usually think better with food around." With that Leon had his secretary order sandwiches.

While they were waiting for the food, Quinn called Luther to find out if he and Jesse had found out anything. Luther updated him on what Jesse had learned. With Grace and Leon watching him intently, Quinn related to them that they now knew, the new dispersant was sprayed on the Logan plume on May 13th. The massive fish kill had occurred a few days later.

Jesse had also checked the weather for that day. He determined there were violent thunderstorms and waterspouts reported in the area of the plume. Dr. Edwards had mentioned that good mixing of the dispersant might be needed for reactions to take place. Waterspouts would certainly have provided that ingredient.

Quinn also relayed that according to a reliable source, Werner Strauss was alone for the majority of the dispersant analysis and he, of course, was dead. His supposed assistant, Tim Gardner, was offsite making out with an underage girl nearly the entire night. Plus, Gardner was now out of the country and not available for questioning.

As lunch arrived, all three were thinking intently. As he passed out the boxed lunches, Leon flipped off the mute on his office TV which was always on CNN or the local news. "Maybe the news will clear our heads," he said jokingly.

As they munched on their sandwiches a news flash came on. "GG Oil announced today that a new dispersant they've been researching has been successful in breaking down one of the larger oil slicks called the Logan Slick. Company spokesman said the slick was completely dissipated and they planned to commence spraying of all the crude oil slicks within the next few days. GG Oil believes this may eliminate the environmental threat to the coastline."

"Oh, shit," Grace and Quinn said in unison. Leon looked alarmed for the first time. Grace stated fiercely, "Leon, we can't let them do this. We have to halt the spraying until we know for sure. Otherwise," her voiced trailed off, and the rest knew exactly what she was thinking. The plague would be spread over such a wide area that it would become totally out of control.

Leon, shaking his head, cautioned, "I know you lived this the past week, and how stressed you are. However, unless we can prove there are human lives at stake, I don't know how we can raise the flag quite yet."

Grace pleaded, "Why don't we request Werner Strauss's body be exhumed?"

"Request it on what grounds?" retorted Leon.

Quinn, trying another tact, argued, "You realize even if there are no immediate human deaths, if plants and most species of fish and animals die off, humans will soon begin dying for lack of food, or worse, killing one another for what food is left."

Leon could feel a heartburn attack coming. He rubbed his temples hoping to avoid a migraine he knew wasn't far behind. Leon pondered, "All right. Let's take a step back. We should be able to find next of kin for Werner Strauss, and try to persuade he or she request an autopsy be performed. That may be tough but doable. Trying to find out about the four alleged bodies Homeland Security has will be far more difficult, but we have to try."

There was silence in the room. Finally Leon concluded, "Here's what I propose. Grace, you and I will set up a meeting at 2:00 PM with the executive editor and the publisher. If they will commit, we'll go front page with this story. My bet is they'll want something on human deaths, or at least something more solid on plant and animal risks before they agree to that. Quinn, I'd like you to get with the rest of your team to pursue an autopsy on Strauss and finding out what you can on the other bodies." Grace and Quinn nodded their agreement.

"We've got to move fast if we're to stop GG Oil from more spraying," admitted Leon. "Let's get moving." Quinn was already headed out the door.

Chapter 42 - June 9, 2010 – 2:00 PM

Quinn arrived at Luther's mission about 2:00PM. Jesse was already there. By computer Quinn and Jesse started researching Werner Strauss's death via newspaper articles. They determined the funeral home that received his body, and decided to call them. Jesse said "Let me do the talking. I'm getting pretty good at this."

Jesse dialed up the number and asked for the funeral home director. Jesse again used his FBI alias of Lt. Charles Romex. After a brief discussion Jesse found out that the only supposed living relative was a nephew named Raymond Strauss from Philadelphia, and that he had requested no autopsy be performed and an immediate burial. No embalming was performed, and therefore there was no viewing and no actual funeral service. The director commented that Werner must have been a recluse because Raymond Strauss and one other man, whose name the director couldn't recall, were the only ones at the burial.

Quinn then started a search on the name Raymond Strauss. His intent was to call Raymond Strauss personally, and try to convince him to exhume the body. He couldn't believe what he found. Raymond Strauss had died in a car accident a year ago on May 5, 2009.

Jesse mocked, "Well, Quinn. Now it looks like we've got ghosts involved in this case."

Yeah," Quinn scoffed. "If we don't stop the oil plume spraying, ghosts may be all that's left around here."

Jesse countered, "Seriously, if that wasn't Raymond Strauss, then who do you suppose filled out the paperwork and was actually at the Werner Strauss burial?"

"My bet would be on someone from Homeland Security."

Jesse, not being used to all the pressure, groaned, "Hey, Quinn. It's almost dinnertime and Luther's about ready with a spaghetti meal for the mission folks. What do you say we take a break and get some grub?"

"That sounds good to me. I'll check out the hall to see if they need any help setting up."

*****

Homeland Security agents Harbaugh, his partner Swatkowski, and a new hire in training, Randall Dobson, pulled up to the Bayou Mission just about the time Quinn was entering the dining room. Harbaugh had the highest seniority and therefore was the lead man for this exercise. He was under instructions from Director Simmons to check out the place and determine if further investigation was justified. Harbough's interpretation of this was to "shake it down" and he loved to intimidate people.

As they approached the door to the mission, Harbaugh ordered, "Ok squad. Let's take this place apart. Dobson, I'm going to show you how we get the scum of the earth's attention by instilling fear in them."

Dobson didn't look so sure and added, "I read the info sheet on this place and it's supposed to be a mission providing a place of shelter and rehabilitation for the homeless and others down on their luck. The guy in charge, a Reverend Brown, has a reputation for really helping the communities he's worked in."

Harbaugh rolled his eyes and countered, "Dobson, here's where experience comes in. I don't bother with the rap sheets. Furthermore, if you go by the manuals on engagement and protocol, you'll get yourself seriously hurt. You move in, make a swift on-the-spot assessment of the situation, then react accordingly. I want you to stay out of the way and just take notes on how we in the field do things."

Dobson shook his head and took a deep breath. Swatkowski just grinned.

Without bothering to knock, Harbaugh pushed open the door and the three agents barged in. They entered a large room where ragged-looking people were filing in for dinner. A long table was being spread with soup and salad, and a card table had been set with a large bowl of spaghetti with some thin sauce on the side.

Harbaugh boomed out, "Homeland Security! We're going to inspect this place for drugs and illegal booze. Anyone who interferes will be arrested."

A voice from behind the food table called out, "Mr. Brown, can you help us please?"

Then Harbaugh noticed Quinn, who had just entered the room, standing off to the side and said, "Well, I'll be damned. I guess they let all kinds of riff raff into this shithole." Harbaugh motioned to Dobson, "See what I mean. They're all scum and hiding something for sure."

Luther Brown came from behind a curtain that separated the main room from the kitchen. As he rounded the corner, he flipped on the surveillance cameras with audio he'd had installed. Not all the residents were harmless, and he knew from experience it was a worthwhile precaution. The cameras and mikes were well hidden.

Luther had on a full length sauce-stained white apron covering his regular smock. He had on a chef's hat that made him look especially comical. He had a big grin which showed off a mouthful of white teeth that looked especially shiny against his dark black skin. "Gentlemen," he said with a friendly voice, "we'd be honored to have you join us for dinner. We were about to say grace. Everyone here has a chore to do, either cooking, serving, or cleaning up. But we all take time together to thank the Lord for our food and the chance for a new life."

Dobson was about to thank him since he was hungry and the food did smell pretty good, but Harbaugh replied rudely, "Look, Chef Boy-R-Dee, I don't want any of your slop and we're not here to exchange pleasantries." A scowl started crossing Luther's face.

Just then, an old scruffy man with tattered clothes and a shaggy grey beard, only known by the name of Thomas, shuffled over toward Harbaugh. Thomas said in a wheezing voice, "Why'd ya call him dat name? His name is Mr. Brown and he be a great cook. He da only one round here who help us."

Harbaugh snapped back, "Get out of my face you shitbag." With that he gave the old man a shove that sent him sprawling across the floor, knocking over a leg of the card table and spilling spaghetti and sauce over him and onto the floor.

Swatkowsky gave out a hearty laugh and Harbaugh said out loud, "Now that's where that crap belongs. I'm sure the floor is spotless enough you can just eat off it. Save you washing dishes." He added to Dobson, "You taking notes kid? This is how we get things done." Quinn noted Luther's face tensing up.

With that, a wisp thin boy named Amos, who was about 10 years old with one leg slightly shorter than the other, limped up to Harbaugh. "Missta, why you hurt Thomas like dat?" challenged Amos. "He just getting over his accident. You messed up our dinner too. You gonna pay for dat?"

Harbaugh got red in the face and yelled, "You smart ass kid. You need to learn some manners." With that he backhanded Amos across the face so hard he knocked him over whacking his forehead on a chair as he fell over. Quinn looked at Luther and noticed Luther's right eye beginning to twitch. Quinn, remembering Jesse's warning, backed up a few steps.

What happened next was beyond belief. All Quinn remembered was a blurr as Luther swept past him. Swatkowski seemed frozen and caught a forearm to the chin that knocked him out cold before he hit the floor. Harbough, who started reaching for his gun, partially blocked the first blow but caught a blast to the solar plexus, an elbow to the face, and a karate chop to the neck all in a split second. As Harbaugh started to go down Luther caught him and literally threw him through the closed front door. The opening Harbough's body made as it crashed through the door looked like a vertical crime scene body outline without the spray paint marking.

Luther then picked up Swatkowshi, who was starting to come to, and threw him out through the window. He hit the ground with a thud, groaning weakly. Luther was headed for Dobson, but Amos had scuttled across the floor resting on hands and knees behind Dobson. Thomas shuffled over and gave Dobson a push sending him tripping backwards over Amos's prone body. Luther smiled and said, "Good work, men. It's great to have someone cover your back."

Glaring down at Dobson, Luther added, "I hope you took good notes and take some words of wisdom back with you. You get a lot more help from people by treating them with dignity and respect. There's no place for meanness in the House of the Lord or anywhere else for that matter. You only use force as a last resort. I could have killed those men, but instead I sent Harbaugh backwards through the door at enough of an angle that his skull wouldn't be crushed. He'll be laid up for awhile but he'll live. Swatkowski will be cut up and sore but not much more. Dobson had feared he'd be attending two partners' funerals after his first assignment.

"By the way" continued Luther, "I got all the action on video. Our lives were threatened by someone not displaying or offering an

ID. Plus my residents were physically abused without provocation. I'm sure your ethics board would be enlightened by this, that is if you want to pursue it. I'd recommend this be chalked up to an auto accident. I'll even help make it more believable."

Luther reached over and picked up Dobson by the shoulder. Dobson braced himself for an impact with some portion of the building, but Luther released his grip.

"Hey, Quinn, come on with me, and bring Dobson with you."

With that, Luther opened the front door, which partially fell off its upper hinge. He ambled over to the Homeland Security green government issued Buick sedan. "Quinn, give me a hand, will you?" said Luther over his shoulder. Luther squatted down near the front of the passenger side door. To Quinn he said, "Get the same side near the back and we'll lift her up on her side."

Quinn looked in amazement but did as he was told. Dobson stood there swaying from side to side, still not sure whether he'd soon feel pain in one form or another.

Before Quinn could put his strength in it, the car was already off the ground as Luther grunted with exertion. Quinn helped lift it the rest of the way. The car ended up resting on the driver's side. There was gravel and some larger rocks in the way that scratched and dented that side of the car. Luther walked around to the other side of the car and Quinn backed out of the way. Luther gave the car a shove, and it crashed back on all four wheels, kicking up a cloud of dust. The passenger side hub caps flew off as the car hit the ground. Several nuts and bolts bounced out from under the car and the muffler broke off from its bracket hitting the ground with a screech of metal.

By now Swatkowshi had propped himself up on one elbow in obvious discomfort. Harbaugh still lay on the ground but his eyes were open though not focusing too well. He had wood splinters from the door in his hair and stuck into his jacket and pants. He kind of looked like he'd been next to a tornado. Swatkowshi attempted to object to their cars demise, but Dobson walked quickly over, waving his hands together and shaking his head afraid of antagonizing Luther any further.

Luther, brushing the dirt off his hands, said calmly, "I know you boys are anxious to be on your way. So I'll have the kitchen fix you up some food in 'to go' boxes. That way you can eat on the way."

Dobson, who had lost his appetite long ago, said, "Thank you Mr. Brown. That's very thoughtful of you." Luther just nodded.

In a few moments a bag appeared with three foam cartons of food. Luther retrieved the agents' guns, unloaded them and tossed them into the trunk, slamming it shut. He then asked Thomas to pull the car around so the agents could get in more easily. Thomas smiled, put the car in reverse and floored it, backing up into a gnarled oak tree, crushing the bumper and putting a good-sized dent in the trunk lid. "Oops." he said.

Two of the residents helped lay Harbough in the backseat. He was in obvious pain. They also helped Swatkowski into the front seat, reclining it as far as it would go so he could lay back. Dobson drove off. The left rear wheel wobbled as they drove away with the muffler scrapping along the road. They sure didn't look like they could secure much of the homeland, for that day anyway.

Chapter 43 - June 9, 2010 – 7:00PM

The southern regional Homeland Security medical office in Chattanooga, Tennessee got a call from director James Simmons about 7:00 PM. Simmons requested they conduct an autopsy on four bodies that were inducted on June 2nd. They were identified only as "Simmons Case" and the accompanying records folder was stamped "Secret". A Jerrus Plank took the call. Jerrus was not the regular medical examiner, Isaac Ternbill, but filled in when Ternbill was on vacation.

"These bodies have been here over a week," chided Plank, not realizing who he was talking to. "It's always hurry up and wait, then a panic at the last minute. I wish the powers to be would get their act together."

"I am the powers to be," growled Simmons. "I'm Director James Simmons, and you better get your act together," warned Simmons with a distinct tone of annoyance.

"Sorry, sir," was all Plank could muster.

"I need cause of death established on all four bodies, and I need it tonight. If you have to work overtime, so be it. Just get it done." With that statement Simmons hung up.

"Shit," Plank yelled out loud. "Kravitz, get your dead ass over here. We've got a hot job and we can't leave until it's done." Lonnie Kravitz was Plank's assistant for the night.

Kravitz assembled the surgical tools they'd need while Plank started the paperwork. They were actually contractors for Homeland Security and worked out of an old lab in the basement of Mercy Hospital, an older facility in downtown Chattanooga.

Plank finished up the boiler plate form, realizing they knew next to nothing about the four males they were about to cut open. They had no name, no address, and no country of origin. Time of death had been estimated on the incoming paperwork. Since death location was outside territorial waters in a ship of unknown origin, Plank wasn't even sure he should be the one conducting the autopsy. But he had his orders, so he continued.

Plank suggested since they had four bodies to do in less than five hours, they bypass some of the formalities for the moment. Kravitz just shrugged his shoulders and commented they better pick up the pace since he had no intention of staying into third shift.

"At least we won't be interrupted by the cleaning crew," retorted Plank. "They got cut back to cleaning every other day as a cost savings."

They rolled the first body out of its refrigerated chamber and slid it onto a gurney. Kravitz elaborated, "This guy must have been on a crash diet. He sure feels light for his size."

They rolled the gurney onto the scales which automatically subtracted the gurney's weight from the measured value giving the body's weight. The body's weight measured 104.6 lbs. The body's length was 5'11". Plank wrote down this information along with "Hispanic" for the nationality. He estimated the age to be 35.

Both Plank and Kravitz visually inspected the body for any evidence of abrasions, wounds, or other trauma. Nothing was evident. Kravitz commented, "That's strange. I thought this was some kind of drug bust. This guy certainly shows no evidence of a struggle."

Plank advised, "Let's proceed to an incision to open the chest cavity."

Although they had on rubber gloves, neither Plank or Kravitz bothered to wear a face mask. They had on lab coats, but they wore them with open collars. Plank made a six-inch incision down the middle of the chest. As he started to spread open the chest cavity, a reddish brown fog-like mist drifted out of the incision.

"What the hell?" murmured Kravitz who was standing right next to Plank.

Plank, who was trying to peer into the chest cavity, got his face coated with the mist. Plank stumbled backwards blinking his eyes. "Jesus Christ!" blurted Plank. "I can't see a damned thing. This shit is sticky. Help me to the wash station."

Kravitz realized the mist was still escaping from the body and drifting towards him and Plank. He waved his hands in the air trying to break up the fog, but in doing so got it all over his gloves and lab coat. Some stuck to his neck. "Ah, shit," swore Kravitz. He grabbed Plank's arm and headed toward the emergency shower.

The emergency shower was in one corner of the room surrounded by shoulder high walls on three sides. Kravitz guided Plank into the room. It had a large shower head with a pull chain which when pulled was supposed to provide a full pressure, high flush of water to rinse off any skin-threatening chemicals.

Not bothering to undress, Kravitz jerked the shower chain. The shower had not been used in years, and regular safety testing had been skipped. The chain was rusty and Kravitz pulled it so hard it broke in two. "God Dammit!" yelled Kravitz.

"What's wrong? Why ain't we getting flushed?" snarled Plank.

"The fucking chain broke. Hold on while I grab a chair to reach the pull lever," snapped Kravitz. "Are your eyes burning?" he yelled over his shoulder as he rushed back toward his desk.

"Not really," snorted Plank. "I feel a warm sensation but that's it. I just can't see. Everything is cloudy like I'm looking through a film of red/brown crap." In his haste to get something to reach the pull lever, it didn't register to Kravitz that he felt a warm sensation in his neck where the mist contacted his skin.

Kravitz rolled his desk chair over to the shower. He centered it under the lever, stepped up and pulled. The force of the water almost knocked him off the chair and he wobbled back and forth trying to gain his balance. The tile floor suddenly got slippery as the water hit the floor. Kravitz overcompensated, and the chair took off like it was possessed. Kravitz's feet flew up in the air, sending him crashing onto the floor, hitting his head full force. Plank was looking directly into the shower of water to flush his face and eyes and nearly got run over by the chair.

"Kravitz, you asshole" screeched Plank. "This ain't a damn swimming pool. You trying to perfect your half gainer or was that your attempt at a cannon ball?" Kravitz didn't answer.

Plank could finally see more clearly and realized Kravitz wasn't moving. "Ah, shit," Plank moaned. He started to run to the phone, but his shoes were now coated with a mixture of water and the film that he had just flushed off his face. The combination was about as slippery as ice and with the second step he slipped falling head first into the wall. He knocked himself unconscious which turned out to be a blessing since he never felt the intense pain caused by the microbes consuming his lungs.

Chapter 44 - June 10, 2010 – 5:30 AM

⸻

Elvira Monez was always the first in the lab, arriving at 5:30 AM on the dot. Expecting to get Plank's carryover from the night before, she headed toward her desk. Something didn't seem right. All the lights were on, although the cleaning crew didn't always turn them off. She forgot this was the first week of the new cleaning schedule. At first, she didn't note the gurney with the body stationed in the center of the lab. But then she saw it.

"What the hell?" she murmured to herself. She headed cautiously over to the gurney. Everything seemed normal except for the incision in the chest. Plank wasn't the best technically, but he was strict about keeping the lab in the same condition he found it. Leaving a body unattended was certainly not like Plank.

She headed back to her desk to get the carryover record. There was none. She slowly swung around, navigating the lab with her eyes. She spotted Plank's body crumpled up against the far wall and immediately broke out into a cold sweat. She hurried over toward him and then almost fainted when she saw the leg of a second body partially protruding from the emergency shower room door. She burst toward the phone on her desk and dialed the internal 911 number.

Because of the time of the morning, it took almost fifteen minutes for the emergency response team to arrive. By then other first shift employees were arriving and soon the scene turned into utter confusion. The response team, consisting of two firemen and a paramedic, quickly determined that both men were dead. Kravitz died of an apparent broken neck. Plank on the other hand had a nasty gash on his head, but they felt it shouldn't have been fatal.

Since normally people brought to the lab were already dead, those present weren't prepared to handle someone dying here. There also was the issue with the body on the gurney, which was ripening by the minute adding an unpleasant aroma to the morbid scene. They desperately needed someone to take charge of the situation.

With all the distractions, no one noticed the reddish-brown footprint stain near the emergency shower doorway, or the reddish-brown coloration around the air conditioning return vent. The dying here was not over.

Chapter 45 - June 10, 2010 – 7:55 AM

Charles Loman, the director of Mercy Hospital, arrived in his office at 7:55 AM. Before he opened his Starbucks coffee, he noticed he had ten messages on his answering machine. Before he could answer the first one, a group of six people pounded on his door. The group included the safety manager, the director of security, the emergency response team, and the morgue director.

"We've got an emergency and need a decision on how to proceed," declared the Security Director who apparently was the self-appointed spokesman for the group.

"What's the emergency," groaned Loman. The group quickly filled him in on what they knew so far, which really wasn't all that much.

By the time the group finished their commentary, Loman felt like his head was being crushed in a vice. "Ok, look, let's set up a meeting in twenty minutes. I want the head of all pertinent departments in attendance. Also, except for the body on the gurney, no one is to touch anything in the lab until we've determined a plan of action. Have someone put the body back in cold storage. I'm going to contact Homeland Security Director Simmons. This was his baby to start with, so I want him to know we have a problem. He may want to conference in on our meeting." The group headed out to grab a conference room and alert the appropriate people.

After three tries and an argument with Director Simmons's secretary, Loman finally got to talk to Homeland Security Director Simmons. After hearing the story, Simmons was furious. "You mean to tell me I request a simple autopsy, and you guys can't deliver? I'll remember this when contract renewal time comes up. I need answers now."

Loman was getting pissed. "Listen," Loman hissed. "You might need them now, but you're not going to get them until we sort out what happened. I've got two employees dead and I don't know if I have a suicide, a murder, an accident, or all or none of the above. I can't proceed with anything until I get an ok from the police. They're just now arriving on the scene."

Simmons wasn't used to being put off but decided to back off slightly. "I am sorry about your people, and I'm sure you're under a lot of stress. But if you don't get me some answers quickly you're going to end up with all kinds of help you don't really want. Senator Lee requested I get answers on these deaths right away, and he can generate a media circus that I'm sure you don't want to deal with. Is there a chance you could do an autopsy on one of the other bodies while you're waiting for police clearance on the one that was started by Plank and Kravitz?"

Loman pondered this for a moment. "I suppose," sighed Loman, "since the other bodies haven't been touched, it shouldn't have any impact on the police investigation. I'm sure the regular lab will be off limits for awhile, but perhaps we could perform the autopsy in an adjacent lab. I'll have to see if our medical examiner will be willing to do this."

Simmons cautioned, "Please impress upon him the urgency of this autopsy and the negative consequences if it's not expedited."

"I'll do that," snorted Loman. "By the way we're having a meeting in about five minutes to develop a plan of action. Do you want to participate?"

Simmons had a full calendar, but decided this took priority. "Yes" he answered. Loman said he'd have his secretary forward the phone in number in about two minutes.

*****

By 8:20 the 25-seat conference room was filled and people were standing along the walls. Loman opened the meeting, requesting introductions for all those present. Loman then had the local police detective assigned to the case, Detective Rollins, go over the protocol to be followed by all. Director Simmons called in just as the detective began. Detective Rollins was noticeably agitated that Homeland Security was already involved. Rollins wanted to completely photograph and check the lab for fingerprints, as well as request no one enter the lab unless cleared by him. He also wanted an autopsy of both bodies ASAP.

Loman then had Elvira Monez summarize what she saw when she arrived at 5:30 AM, and the response team reiterate what they found. An action plan was laid out that seemed acceptable to all, with the exception of Director Simmons. Simmons asked that one of his other three bodies be released for autopsy, and it be performed in an adjacent lab today. Detective Rollins was not in favor of this and wanted autopsies to be performed on both Plank and Kravitz immediately. After several minutes of discussion, Detective Rollins finally relented with the understanding that the Plank and Kravitz autopsies would be next up. The meeting concluded with everyone assigned at least one task.

Loman called the day shift medical examiner, a Thomas Moran, hoping he wouldn't be too adverse to doing the autopsy in the much smaller lab adjacent to the regular lab. This just wasn't Loman's day. Moran, a crotchety old guy who sensed the world was out to get him, raised holy hell.

"Not just no, but hell no! There's no room there. The body's got to be moved back and forth, plus all the instruments are in the other lab."

Loman took a deep breath in between gulping down two extra-strength headache meds and replied, "Tom, give me a list of what you need, and I'll have a new set of instruments brought down from supply. I'll have an orderly stand by with you to bring the body and anything else you need immediately. I agree the lab is small, but please work with me on this. We're under the gun to get this right away."

"All right, all right," griped Moran, "but you owe me one big time."

Chapter 46 - June 10, 2010 – 1:00PM

J ust after lunch Moran was ready to begin the autopsy on the second "Simmons" labeled body. The orderly, Sam Stiggins, picked up the needed instruments from supply and brought in the body. Since the scale was in the other lab they couldn't get a precise weight. Moran was going to estimate the weight based on height, which was 5'8", and muscular build. However, Stiggins indicated the body was really light, probably not much over 100 lbs.

"You sure?" asked Moran.

"Yep," answered Stiggins, "Seemed strange to me, too."

Moran started the tape recorder and put in all information verbally. Moran was dressed properly with a mask, tightly buttoned lab coat and gloves. Stiggins just had on normal work clothes. The plan was that he was to stay out of the way and only get whatever Moran needed that wasn't available in the lab. He sat on a stool about ten feet away.

Moran visually inspected the body and noted a large gash on the right leg, which was bandaged. The leg wasn't broken and the laceration would not have been life threatening. There did not appear to be any other physical damage to the body. Moran noted his observations verbally. He then stated that he was going to make a chest incision to check internal organs. Stiggins, who looked like he was about to nod off, suddenly showed renewed interest.

Moran made a six-inch long incision just below the breast bone. As he spread open the tissue, he looked up at Stiggins, hoping to gross him out and sneered, "I always love this part."

As Moran watched Stiggins's face, he noted his expression change from a passive smile to a look of fear. "You better watch what the hell you're doing," gasped Stiggins.

Moran looked down and was faced with a thick reddish brown fog emanating from the incision. "What the hell is this?" sputtered Moran. "Stiggins get a container to capture this stuff…now!"

Stiggins flew off his stool looking around the lab. Nothing was in sight. He slammed open the door to the hallway thinking he'd get something from the lab across the hall. The door stop at the base of the door dropped down holding the door open. Stiggins didn't realize the lab was a "special clean lab" that meant it was pressurized slightly to insure outside air did not enter. With the exit door now open, the air inside the lab circulated to the hallway. To Moran's dismay, the fog followed the airflow escaping into the hall.

"Stiggins," yelled Moran, "Close the God Damn door."

It was too late as Stiggins was already in the other lab. Several people walking down the hall were attracted to the disturbance, and walked right through the mist which coated their arms and faces. Stiggins came running out of the lab with a large glass beaker, and stumbled into the group who were vigorously rubbing their faces and arms trying to remove the sticky stuff. He got some on his arms as well.

Moran was still yelling for someone to close the door. Some of the mist had gotten on his ears and he had backed away from the body, ripped off his mask, and was trying to wash off the residue.

Moran howled, "You're too late with that beaker. Get those people outside isolated. Call security to cordon off the hall. I don't know what this is, but it's scaring the shit out of me!"

Stiggins was momentarily frozen, not knowing what to do

first. Moran hollered, "Move!" Stiggins shrieked at the three people outside to come into the lab immediately. They did and he closed the door. He then called the internal 911 not knowing who else to call. Moran yanked the phone from Stiggins and told the dispatcher that there was an environmental release in hallway 5 DD that needed to be contained immediately. He slammed the phone down. Stiggins noticed a reddish brown stain on the earpiece.

Moran then called Loman and lambasted him for not telling him what to expect. Loman pleaded innocence since he didn't have the faintest idea what was going on. Loman decided right then to call Director Simmons a second time.

Meanwhile, Loman demanded all five of the people that came in contact with the mist be quarantined in the lab. "This is bullshit," bellowed Moran even though he knew Loman was right.

"Ok, people," moaned Moran, "We're stuck here for the time being. Let's wash this stuff off into a container so we can keep a sample. I doubt if this is a concern, but it's best to play it safe in case HIV or anything like that is involved."

Loman called Director Simmons again, but this time Simmons was in a terrorist status meeting and couldn't be pulled out. His secretary promised to get him as soon as he came out of the meeting. While he waited to hear from Simmons, Loman decided he better review the emergency contamination containment procedures just in case this incident escalated and he needed to cover his ass.

While all this was going on, Lt. Rollins and his police team were taking pictures of the main lab initially assuming it was a crime scene. Because the lab was sealed off, they were oblivious to the commotion occurring in the adjacent lab. As they photographed the scene, they did note a reddish-brown footprint not far from where Plank's body was found. Later they also took pictures of the A/C return vent which had a similar colored stain, although no one made the connection.

At about 2:10 Rollins got a call from Loman telling him that an incident had occurred in the lab next door. Loman described what had happened and it dawned on both of them that the four specially marked "Simmons" bodies might actually be a factor in the investigation. It could even be a terrorist biological warfare plot. Loman indicated he'd tried to contact Simmons again, but Simmons hadn't returned his call. Rollins told him he'd be right up and they'd not let Simmons rest until he talked to them.

By 2:15 Rollins and Loman were on hold while Simmon's secretary went looking for him. Rollins told her this was a suspected terrorist plot which at least forced her into action. They heard cursing in the background as Simmons came on the line.

"This better be good 'cause now you've got my boss pissed."

Loman, whose headache had reached critical mass, lost it. "This ain't good, it's bad, real bad, and I demand to know what the fuck is going on. A fog came out of the second of your bodies while our medical examiner was doing the autopsy. Five people got red, sticky shit all over them, and I don't know how serious this is. Right now all five are quarantined in that small lab. I need answers."

There was silence from Simmons who had a creepy feeling that he was in deep shit.

"Well?" screamed Loman.

Simmons finally answered, "I'm being perfectly frank with you. I don't know what this is."

Something suddenly hit Rollins and he spoke for the first time, "We got some pictures from the lab of a footprint with a reddish stain and a suspicious red stain on the air conditioner vent. The footprint seemed to match Plank's shoe although we haven't had time to confirm that. What if this fog-like stuff came out of the first body and got over Plank and maybe Kravitz too?"

Chills ran down Loman's neck. "I'd better warn Moran and the others," he panted. As he was about to put Simmons on hold so he could call on the other line, an emergency light began flashing and an emergency siren sounded in the hall.

"Oh, shit," bellowed Loman, "we've got an emergency in the backup lab." He put the phone on conference and called the lab.

Moran answered in a panic, "We've got two people in intense pain and I'm not feeling good myself. We need help down here now!"

Chapter 47 - June 10, 2010 – 12:30 PM

While the emergency at Mercy hospital was unfolding, Grace and Leon met with the executive editor, Mark Schuler, and publisher, Randall Ursage. Leon took the lead in presenting their story and periodically asked Grace to clarify some of the facts as they knew them.

When they finished, Schuler and Ursage eyed one another and shook their heads. Schuler was the first to respond, "That's one hell of a story. Do you have any confirmation on human deaths?"

"No," Leon answered, "but we're working on the next of kin lead for GG's expert chemist that died."

Ursage weighed in, "So the only concrete information saying we have a potential virus outbreak of some kind is from a rogue scientist."

"Dr. Edwards is far from a rogue scientist. He was a highly respected researcher," Grace replied defensively.

Ursage interrupted, "Yeah, but the 'was' is what concerns me. What if he's carrying a chip on his shoulder from the past? I don't want our paper to come across as one of those tabloids. Leon, what's your recommendation?"

Leon took a deep breath then responded, "I have reservations, but my gut tells me Grace and her group is definitely onto something. Until the announcement by GG Oil, I would have waited for more substantiation. But now I think we should pull the trigger and go front page headline.

Grace was astonished but tried to keep calm. Schuler and Ursage conferred privately for a moment and then came back, "Go with it. We hope to hell you're right about this or all are asses will be hung out to dry."

Leon and Grace thanked them and headed for the door to prepare their headline story for the evening edition. Leon also got the ok to provide a story feed to CNN and CNBC. Grace quickly called Quinn to inform him they finally had a breakthrough and were proceeding with the story. She emphasized that he tell the rest, and set up a conference call with the team at 3:00 PM to assemble the latest input. Grace emphasized, "The story must hit hard and have as many facts as possible. We've got to blow them away with so many scenarios they can't answer them all without stopping the spraying, at least temporarily."

Grace and Leon had the story draft ready by the 3:00 PM call. The call proved to be raucous since nearly everyone had news. The most significant input came from Luther who exclaimed, "I think we found the four lost bodies. I just got a call from my cleaning contacts in Chattanooga. The downtown hospital there, called Mercy Hospital, is in emergency lockdown mode from a suspected environmental release. The release came during autopsies of at least two bodies. An unknown number of people are quarantined and some deaths are suspected. No one is releasing any information to the public." Grace and Leon knew right away they would add this to their story.

Dr. Edwards had even more chilling news. He now believed insect and plant species were at risk. He introduced fleas onto an infected mouse and all fleas, as well as the mouse, were dead within a five-hour period. He only checked a few flowering annual plants, but those had already wilted after exposure for 12 hours. Edwards said he was more convinced than ever that this was the cause of the Great Mass Extinction, and it could already have started again right there in Louisiana. "It must be contained immediately," he said emphatically.

Quinn and Jesse concluded with the facts that no autopsy was performed on Werner Strauss and the person who supposedly signed the "No Embalming Request" had in reality died a year earlier.

Grace and Leon completed their story which even they had to admit was damn good. The headline read:

Mass Extinction Feared From Oil Spill – Deaths Already Starting

With a smile of satisfaction, Leon called CNN and CNBC providing them a summary of their article. The response was like the strike from a bolt of lightning. Up until now it had been a rather non-newsworthy day. This story changed everything. The major networks called shortly afterwards requesting interviews. Leon had intentionally left out names of the ranking officials that appeared to be covering up the story, although he did mention Homeland Security and the suspicions that a Louisiana senator was involved. Everyone assumed that was Senator Lee. Leon did refer to the investigative group as the 'Tidal Surge' and included their names. By 9:00 PM that evening Leon would realize he should not have identified the Tidal Surge members.

Chapter 48 - June 10, 2010 – 5:00 PM

W ithin the hour Southern Regional Director Simmons got a call from his boss, Charles Oman the National Homeland Security Director. Oman wanted to know who this Tidal Surge Group was and what the hell was going on.

Simmons answered defensively, "We've researched the names and they include an unemployed fisherman, a backwoods female newspaper reporter, a Berkeley scientist fired from MIT, a liberal, bible-thumbing Baptist minister who's trying to make a name for himself, and a so-called medical expert who in fact is a veterinarian. Now do you think we should really believe them? I say we put the screws to them and they'll go away."

"Well," exclaimed Oman, "the news is having a field day with this and the story is compelling even if it is a pack of lies. Furthermore, what is going on at that Hospital and how did they find out about it? Is there any truth to that expert chemist's death and burial? What's being done with the drums of fluid from the tug that was brought in? Damn it, Simmons, I'm being deluged with questions and I look like I'm totally incompetent. You better get answers within the hour or you're going to be next in line for the soup kitchen." With that Oman hung up.

By now Simmons was sweating profusely. Before he could take some meds, his red phone rang again. This time it was Senator Lee. Lee was in an equally foul mood. Lee lambasted, "Simmons, you professed you had this under control. I'd hate to see when you claim things are out of control. I've had calls from the major networks, and I'm denying all knowledge. Trouble is that damned Luther Brown and his sidekick, something Carter, met with us. I knew they'd be trouble. You were going to take care of them or did you forget that promise as well? Say something, damn it!"

Simmons was losing it, but suddenly had a thought. "I'll bet that bastard Beauregard Calhoun had something to do with that tug. He's always bragging about covering all the bases. He's one slimy son-of-a-bitch."

"I don't trust him either," retorted Lee. "The only one he gives a shit about is himself. Let's get him on the phone right now!"

Simmons put Lee on conference and dialed Calhoun's private line. Calhoun picked up on the third ring. "Senator Lee and Director Simmons, what a pleasant surprise," crooned Calhoun.

"Pleasant my ass," fumed Simmons.

"Look you bastard," exploded Lee. "Have you been watching the news?"

"Whoa, gentlemen," coaxed Calhoun. "What's all the fuss? I don't have much use for the news. I'd much rather watch a ballgame, which is exactly what I'm doing."

"Well, you better join the real world, Calhoun," exclaimed Simmons. "That tug you goaded me into checking out had four bodies on it, and autopsies on the first two released some toxins that has already killed two people and four more are on their death bed. I'm betting you had something to do with it. Now the news is suggesting there is a mass extinction of life about to grab us by the short hairs. What happened to the tug's four crewmen and what the hell was in the drums on the tug's deck?"

Senator Lee chimed in, "Calhoun, if this is for real, you're going down in the history books as the mass murderer of all of Louisiana. By the way, I'm personally putting your land deal on hold."

That got Calhoun's attention. "Listen, boys," sputtered Calhoun. "Why are you all over my ass? What makes you think I know anything about a tug, its crew, or its cargo?"

"Because you're a heartless bastard!" yelled Simmons.

"You chicken shits sound like a bunch of caged rats trying to escape the proverbial sinking ship." snarled Calhoun. "I was a good ole boy when you needed votes. But times are a changing, aren't they. I've had enough of your abuse." With that Calhoun hung up, leaving Lee and Simmons staring at their phones.

Lee finally retorted, "In politics that's what we call a non-denial denial."

"Meaning what?" asked Simmons.

"Meaning Calhoun didn't outright deny he had anything to do with the tug. I bet he did but he just won't admit it. He probably figured we were taping the call."

"Were you?" questioned Simmons.

"Damn right," was Lee's answer. Simmons made a mental note not to trust the 'esteemed' senator ever again.

"So what's the plan, Simmons?" asked Lee.

"I don't know, but I need answers fast," replied Simmons. "The only thing I do know is if I go down, you're going down with me," warned Simmons.

After a long pause, Lee proposed with an ice-like voice, "First thing I suggest is we both get a hold of the Coast Guard to force them to analyze the stuff in those drums if they haven't already done so. If there is any truth to that news release, we better emphasize they use full HAZMAT gear."

"Second, let's try smearing this 'Tidal Surge Group' to make it look like they're just trying to get publicity. That shouldn't be hard since they're a bunch of nobodies anyway."

"We'll try that, but I wouldn't underestimate them," responded Simmons. "They've asked some damn pointed questions and probably have some cards they're not playing just yet. To be honest with you, I'm not convinced they're wrong."

With that statement, Senator Lee felt stomach acid welling up in his throat and nearly gagged. "Maybe it's time we find out what GG Oil's real story is," sputtered Lee. "I'm not so sure they've been up front with us on this from the get go."

Chapter 49 - June 10, 2010 – 6:00 PM

A ll the major networks wanted what resembled a live press conference with the Tidal Surge Group. The conference was scheduled for 6:00 PM at the city town hall, which was actually a renovated former high school auditorium. A video feed from Berkeley was hastily set up by the local San Francisco NBC News affiliate so Dr. Edwards could take part. Much to his chagrin, everyone agreed Quinn should be the spokesperson for the group. A group statement was generated which Quinn was to read, and then a question/answer session would follow.

The statement was handed out as everyone entered the meeting room. Word had gotten out fast, and many of the town folks showed up as well as news media representatives. They ran out of seats and statement copies, having not accounted for such high interest. The room took on the look of a true back woods town meeting.

The meeting was to begin promptly at 6PM. However, people were still filing in. By 6:10 Quinn, who was at the podium, could tell the news people, seated in a reserved section in front, were becoming agitated. "Ladies and Gentlemen, can I please have your attention," announced Quinn. "I apologize for the limited seating, but this was arranged rather hastily and we were only expecting members of the press. You all are welcome, but please be as quiet as possible."

"We need to get started. I am Quinton Jones. Like many of you,

I am presently out of work and have been since the moratorium on gulf fishing was put in place. But that is not why I'm here. Myself and other concerned citizens formed a group we named the Tidal Surge. I will now read our statement:

Concerned citizens from several states have determined that a possible link exists between the Deep Water Horizon oil leak, a new dispersal agent that was sprayed on the Logan Oil slick, and wildlife and human deaths. In fact, we believe a microbe type virus from primordial times has been released from the crude oil from which most, if not all, present day earth life forms have no immunity. If unchecked, this virus will destroy life as we know it."

There was a collective gasp from the audience.

"Therefore, we request authorities force the cessation of oil slick spraying with this new dispersant until a comprehensive analysis can be completed. Furthermore, we implore the United States Government and all worldwide health organizations coordinate scientific cooperation to evaluate this microbe and find an antibody or cure to protect all life forms.

Finally, we believe Homeland Security and GG Oil have intentionally, or perhaps unintentionally, undertaken a cover-up of this potential worldwide disaster. However, because of the urgency of this issue, we request establishing blame be set aside and all emphasis be directed toward finding a cure.

With utmost urgency,

Tidal Surge"

As Quinn concluded, there was a lot of whispering in the audience. "I'll take questions now," announced Quinn. Immediately hands from all those in the front row shot up.

"I'll just go from left to right," stated Quinn, feeling intimidated by the response. "Please stand and identify yourself as you ask questions. I'll repeat the question so everyone can hear." With that he pointed toward a fashionably-dressed, red-headed woman on the far left.

"I'm Wanda Staroni of CNN News. Why do you believe there is any danger, and to what extent are the citizens here exposed?"

Quinn repeated the question, then responded, "First, I want to be very clear. This will not remain a localized event. We believe, possibly within a short time period, the entire Gulf and East Coast of the United States could be impacted, particularly if spraying with the new dispersal agent begins in earnest."

A buzz from the crowd ensued.

Quinn gestured his hands to quiet the noise. "Dr. Edwards has completed very preliminary experiments on mice, fish, and some plants. For the animals and fish, death occurred within less than four hours in every case tested."

The crowd reaction renewed.

"We also believe at least seven human deaths have resulted from contact with the microbe," continued Quinn.

Grumbling from the crowd intensified.

Not to be outdone by CNN, the second person from the left jumped up yelling, "I'm Tom Duboise from CNBC. Where have the human deaths occurred, and how do you know they're related?"

Quinn replied, knowing his answer could decide the group's credibility, "I'll be the first to admit we are very early in the investigation and some of our information may seem like circumstantial evidence. But to ignore this could prove catastrophic."

As Quinn was about to continue, Grace, who was manning the news phone hotline that had been setup, walked across the stage and handed a note to Quinn. Quinn hesitated as he read the note, then smiled at Grace.

"The first human death occurred at the GG Oil research laboratory where the head chemist was analyzing mixtures of crude oil from the leak and the new dispersal agent that we're concerned about. He died the night he analyzed the samples. We don't know the cause of death for sure, but he was buried without embalming and without a funeral. This is one of the cover-up concerns. We believe his body should be exhumed and analyzed."

"In addition, there were four bodies removed from a tug boat adrift near the Logan Oil Slick. I just got confirmation from the Coast Guard that these were the same four bodies Homeland Security took to the Mercy Hospital in Chattanooga. An autopsy on the first body was started last night, and the two doing the autopsy were found dead this morning. A second autopsy was started this afternoon and five more people were infected. Two of those have already died and the others are not expected to survive."

There was an even louder, angrier reaction from the audience. All the news media people were now furiously taking notes. Their faces, that moments before had looks of skepticism, now showed serious concern.

The third news reporter jumped up. "I'm Steven Jones from CBS News. Do you know how this is transmitted?"

Quinn surmised, "Our first indication was from an autopsy of a cat that ate some fish from the massive fish kill that came ashore a week ago. When an incision was made to examine the internal organs, a mist rose out of the body. Apparently from the note I just got, this is the same thing that happened during the human autopsies. The mist contains the microbe, and contact with it is fatal."

With that comment, pandemonium erupted from the audience. Yells of, "Why are we only hearing about this now?" were heard along with more derogatory swearing and accusations.

Quinn tried to keep things from getting out of control. "Quiet, please. Please be considerate so we can answer all questions," pleaded Quinn.

Quinn pointed to the fourth news caster who then rose. "I'm Frank York from ABC News. You've implied that Homeland Security instigated a cover-up of this information. What grounds do you have for this accusation?"

Quinn retorted, "I can only say, based on our limited contact with their agents, that Homeland Security confiscated sea life samples I collected from the fish kill before I could have them analyzed. They confiscated the remains of the cat I described earlier before it could be analyzed, and took control of the four tug boat bodies and just now began the autopsies. In addition, the GG chemist's body was buried under strange circumstances. This all could be coincidental but I doubt it. However, as I said before, we must concentrate all efforts on finding an antidote, not assigning blame."

The questions and answers continued for almost another hour. Dr. Edwards presented his theory on the mass extinction and why this crude oil might be different. The entire audience was mesmerized. By 8:30 Quinn was exhausted and the journalists looked haggard as well. Some had already rushed out to get their bylines in. Quinn finally concluded the meeting with another appeal for a united effort from world health organizations.

As Quinn slumped into a chair backstage, Grace came over to congratulate him for a fantastic job. Her enthusiasm was short lived as the news hot line phone rang. After some heated conversations, Grace hung up and told Quinn the news. "That was the Homeland Security National Director. He wants us to attend a closed-door meeting tomorrow at 10:00 AM with Senator Lee, Homeland Security, and GG Oil executives and legal counsel. I think the proverbial shit just hit the fan."

Chapter 50 - June 11, 2010 – 10:00 AM

T he entire Tidal Surge Group, including Quinn, Grace, LeAnn, Luther, Jesse, and Dr. Edwards, who managed to catch a red-eye flight from San Francisco, assembled in the state capital conference room in Baton Rouge.

As expected, Homeland Security arranged the room such that Tidal Surge Group would feel intimidated. The group sat in hard wooden chairs situated a step lower and across from a long mahogany table where all the other attendees were seated. All the others had plush soft leather captain chairs with comfortable arm rests. A stenographer with her stenography machine sat facing the short side of the table. It appeared like an inquisition was about to take place.

Charles Oman, The National Homeland Security Director, opened the meeting. Simmons, the southern regional director, sat next to him. Oman asked for introductions including each person's position.

At their side of the table, in addition to Oman and Simmons, were Senator Lee, Bernard Johnson, the owner and founder of the legal firm of Johnson, Masters, & Clark; several assistants sat behind him although they were not introduced; Silas Thorton III, GG Oil President; Foulton Haverty, GG Oil Head Legal Counsel; and Ronald McAlister, GG Oil Engineering Manager. Ronald Strong,

GG Oil's Chemical Analysis Department Manager, sat behind McAlister, but was not introduced.

The Tidal Surge Group introduced themselves. The only somewhat impressive title belonged to Dr. Edwards. None of the others offered any job titles since they really didn't have any. They simply mentioned what they did for a living. As introductions from their side of the table were completed, Quinn noted condescending sneers on the faces of the assistants behind Johnson.

After the introductions, Oman began, "Mr. Quinn, you presented some interesting hypotheses at your press meeting last night. Of even more concern however, were the numerous accusations directed at Homeland Security and GG Oil. Please enlighten us as to what grounds you have for these accusations."

"If I may interrupt," proclaimed Bernard Johnson, Senator Lee's highly regarded legal counsel, "do you or your group retain legal counsel?"

Quinn answered, "We do not."

"You might need it before we're through here!" blurted out Simmons. Oman gave him the stink eye.

Luther stood up, partly because his chair barely supported his bulk and partly because he wanted to return some of the intimidation. "Gentlemen, and I'm using the term loosely," stated Luther sarcastically looking directly at Simmons, "this meeting is already taking on an adversarial tone and for no good reason. Our group has only had the intention of trying to get to the truth. At almost every turn Homeland Security has taken evidence we collected and hidden it or simply didn't attempt to find results. Can you tell us the real cause of Werner Strauss's death? What were the results of the Crude Oil and dispersant mixture analysis and who did the analysis? Can you tell us what you found from the dead cat's remains? Or how about the liquid inside the drums recovered from the tug boat that was adrift?"

"By the way," added Dr. Edwards anticipating the answer was

they hadn't done it yet, "I'd handle those drums with utmost care as we suspect the virus will be highly concentrated."

"What about the Mercy Hospital deaths and the results of those autopsies?" continued Luther.

The rapid fire questions and forcefulness with which they were asked seemed to momentarily stun the far side of the table. Quinn stood and, with a stare of ice aimed at Oman, concluded, "As I said last night, we are not interested in blame. We only want the truth. If we are correct about this being a deadly microbe, action needs to be taken immediately."

Oman recovered enough to respond, "Let's take your comments one at a time, and hopefully we will put you at ease. Foulton, would you please field the first question."

The GG Oil legal counsel addressed the group, "I'd like to make it clear that Werner Strauss had a history of heart attacks. Mr. Strauss was working with a colleague on the crude oil/dispersant mixture analysis, and it was this person that signed off on the acceptability of the analysis."

Jesse jumped up nearly knocking over his chair and renounced, "Sir, the colleague you mentioned was Timothy Gardner. He was three months out of college, and even worse, he was at his apartment with an underage girl from 6PM to 11PM the night the dispersant analysis was performed. He returned to the lab to find Strauss's body. Unless Strauss had detailed notes on the analysis results, Gardner could not have known whether the dispersant was safe or not. Would you care to comment?"

Thorton glanced at McAlister who looked to Strong. Strong simply shook his head no. Thorton replied, "We'll have to investigate that internally." Oman's face showed his displeasure.

"However," continued Thorton, "we did conduct back-up tests per the analysis protocol the next day. Those results did not show any adverse effects of the dispersant."

"Can you confirm that Strauss followed the protocol precisely?" questioned Quinn.

"If Strauss was actually alone, as you claim, then I'd have to respond with a negative," replied Thorton curtly.

LeAnn took her turn standing and declared, "I conducted the autopsy on the cat Mr. Jones alluded to earlier. I have never seen anything like it. From the outside the cat looked fine. However, all internal organs were gone, consumed by something. As mentioned last night, a fog-like mist came out of the inside of the cat when I made the initial incision. Agent Barlow took the cat's remains before I could do any analysis. However, the residue from the mist was on our air filters, and that's what Dr. Edwards used to conduct his experiments."

"I've heard that the Mercy Hospital deaths occurred from contact with this same type mist. The mist was released when incisions were made in the bodies found on the tug. I urge you to capture some of that mist if you haven't already. Samples will be needed for all kinds of testing."

Director Oman didn't like the way this interrogation was going. It seemed like the Tidal Surge Group had answers to questions he hadn't even asked yet. Grace stood and asked whether they had analyzed the cat's remains.

"Not yet," answered Simmons. Oman's face registered obvious disgust.

"I don't suppose you have results on the contents of the drums, do you?" commented Quinn.

Simmons shook his head no.

Senator Lee had been waiting for his side to take the offensive, but he realized ineptness or stupidity or both prevailed. He figured he better try to salvage his political future by taking the initiative. "Ladies and Gentlemen," he crooned with his deep southern drawl, "I believe we owe these folks our apologies. I believe, Director Simmons, you were approaching this entire incident as if it were a terrorist act. From what I've heard, I believe we may have headed down the wrong trail. I propose we turn our attention to determining if this truly is a microbe or virus or whatever, as Dr. Edwards suggests."

Simmons blinked twice and was about to respond when his boss, Director Oman replied, "I had just come to the same conclusion. We need to get world health involved and brief the President."

"Dr. Edwards and Ms. Roberts, we would appreciate you acting as consultants for the time being to help get our people up to speed." They both consented to help.

Quinn offered, "I have a list of items that we feel should be addressed on a priority basis. They are in order of importance:

1. Discontinue spraying all dispersants, but in particular the new dispersant sprayed on May 13, 2010.
2. Conduct autopsies on the bodies from the Mercy Hospital deaths, capturing and analyzing any emanating mist.
3. Exhume Werner Strauss's body and determine cause of death. This will verify whether the deaths are related or separate incidences.
4. Analyze the fluid in the drums from the tug. Determine if the fluid contains the virus.
5. Release the chemistry of the 'new' dispersant sprayed on May 13th and establish whether the dispersant is a contributor to this event.
6. While all these are going on, mobilize world health organizations and the scientific community to find an antidote."

Director Oman addressed the rest of those at their side of the table, "Do we agree that these are the items we need to work first?"

All heads nodded yes.

"Furthermore," added Oman, "I'm requesting GG Oil not

spray any additional dispersant until we understand its impact. I'll personally sign off on this directive."

GG Oil's legal council confirmed their concurrence.

Grace stood and asked, "Director Oman, how are you planning press coverage on this?"

"I suppose," commented Oman, "we will need daily advisories similar to those held during the Gulf War. I'd like you, Grace, to be point man... err... woman on this."

Grace smiled and answered, "My pleasure."

"I think we're done here," declared Director Oman. "We need to ramp this up to a top priority. We've got a lot of work to do." Oman looked toward Simmons and asserted, "James, we need to put together a going-forward plan. How about we meet back here in say 15 minutes?"

Simmons, who was now rather red faced, simply nodded agreement.

As they left the meeting, the Tidal Surge Group was elated. They finally had accomplished what initially seemed impossible.

***** PART FOUR *****

Chapter 51 - Crunch Time

During the ensuing weeks, Director Oman kept his word. National Disease Control was notified and began mobilizing for a possible pandemic. LeAnn assisted with the autopsies of Plank, Kravitz, and the others that came in contact with the mist, all of whom had died. Except for Kravitz, all bodies contained the dreaded red fog and all had internal organs consumed by the microbe.

Kravitz seemed to be a wild card because the mist did not exit his body nor were his organs consumed. Dr. Edwards theorized that since he died from a broken neck, perhaps this occurred shortly after contact with the virus, and the virus hadn't had enough time to enter his blood stream.

Also, Werner Strauss's body was exhumed. Autopsy revealed he to had been a victim of the virus.

Samples of the mist taken from each of the bodies were distributed to molecular and cellular virologist experts around the world. Researchers were gearing up for an all-out war. However, traditional evaluation efforts were hampered because hosts did not stay alive long enough to determine whether a given antibiotic or antiviral drug was effective. In fact, no drug tried seemed to quell the spread of the microbe.

Meanwhile, analysis of the contents of the drums from the stricken tug verified the liquid was in fact crude oil from the Deep

Horizon Well leak. GG Oil provided the chemical fingerprinting of the oil which permitted exact identification of its well origin.

Dr. Edwards realized too late that a simple indicator test was needed to verify whether the virus was present in whatever medium they were analyzing. Unfortunately, one of the workers taking samples from the drums came in contact with the crude oil, and didn't realize it. Within an hour he showed symptoms, and was immediately treated. The strongest antibiotics and antiviral medications available were tried. They only prolonged his life for about an extra hour. A subsequent autopsy produced the same mist and organ consumption.

*****

Grace was proving to be an excellent newscaster and point person. Grace provided daily updates to the news media at noon each day. All the evening newscasts carried excerpts from her input. But instead of relishing in the limelight, she realized fame at this price was empty indeed.

The only promising news was that direct contact with the microbe was required for infection to occur. If they could contain it, they would at least have more time to find a cure. However, ominous signs were appearing.

Quinn had been assigned a team of divers to check the reefs near the fish kill as LeAnn had suggested earlier. They found that what had been a diverse reef ecology months before was nearly barren. No reef fish were to be found, and coral and shellfish normally inhabiting the area were either dead or greatly reduced. Currents were not particularly strong in the immediate vicinity, but reefs only a few miles away showed telltale signs of stress. Plankton counts were also way down, meaning sea life in all forms was threatened.

Initially biologists felt land plants and animals were relatively safe, providing the mist that emanated from dead bodies was not released to the environment. It was Dr. Edwards that raised a concern about the burial of the remains from the fish kill several weeks ago, infecting ground water. Without a test for the presence of the microbe, they had to rely on observations of the trees and other plants closest to the dump site.

Unfortunately, plants there were beginning to wither, and adjacent trees were loosing large amounts of leaves. Trying to contain this was proving hopeless. Soon, leaf and grass-sucking insects were found dead, as well as small rodents and other herbivores. Dead birds were being discovered as well. The Death of Life prophecy was unfolding, and it seemed man had neither the ability nor the technology to stop it.

The US economy was beginning to feel the impact as well. Other countries were putting moratoriums on exports of all agricultural products from the US. In addition, travel to the US was dropping rapidly. There was talk overseas of isolating the United States from the rest of the world. As expected, stock prices were tumbling. Repercussions were just beginning, and few seemed to grasp that this calamity would not remain a US only problem for long.

Of particular concern to Dr. Edwards was what happened if the virus-contaminated ground water came to the surface as a spring, or formed a small lake. Would the virus follow the water vapor resulting from natural evaporation? Would it survive in clouds and then return to earth as precipitation? If it did, then the spread of the virus would be accelerated much faster then his original estimates. They desperately needed a method to determine if the virus was present in water.

Chapter 52 - Payback Time

While medical science wrestled with finding a cure, the US Senate established a commission to hold hearings with a mandate to determine who was at fault in this disaster. Tidal Surge had hoped to focus all attention on finding a cure. However, politics being what it is and the news media stoking the controversy, the United States Senate felt compelled to take action.

Senate hearings commenced. As they progressed over the next several weeks, the name Beauregard Calhoun surfaced in numerous testimonies, particularly as it related to the tug boat and its dangerous cargo of infected crude oil.

Beau, along with the rest of the nation, watched the proceedings live on CNN and CNBC. So far Beau had not been subpoenaed to appear in person. However, he sensed that he might soon be on national TV, and his name and reputation would definitely not end up in Louisiana history books in the way he had hoped. Beau became more and more depressed. He was having trouble sleeping, continually vacillating on whether to bring up the existence of the second tug should he be asked to testify.

As he sat in his dining room at 1:00 AM slowly stirring his fifth bourbon and water, a knock on his front door startled him into the real world. His doorman had long since gone home for the evening, and he not only felt, but was totally alone.

As he headed toward the door, he heard the distinct click of the dead bolt lock. In his alcohol-induced, sleep-deprived haze; it occurred to him that he had neglected to activate his alarm system. He turned toward his study on the other side of the house where he kept a loaded 38 revolver. However, he was moving much too slowly, and a hand grabbed his shoulder as he reached the hallway.

"Well, I finally get to meet the speaker on the other end of the phone," said a gruff forceful voice. Beau spun around and looked into a round, rugged face covered with a two day old stubble of beard.

Beau squinted, but had no idea who he was talking to. "Who the hell are you, and get out of my house," Beau yelled, not being one to wilt under pressure.

"Come on, Mr. Calhoun. That's not a southern gentlemen's way of greeting a former business partner. I guess we haven't been properly introduced though. I'm Captain Braun, the tireless captain that piloted your second tug exactly as you requested. Well, almost anyway," added Braun with a twisted smile.

It took Beau a moment for his brain to register, but the fog finally cleared. "You were paid per the agreement along with the generous bonus. Get out!"

"I agree we were paid as advertised" sneered Braun, "but the situation has changed. I figure the value of that tug's cargo is significantly more than you let on. Plus, if you believe the news, the whole world could be in danger, and you just might be the scapegoat primed for lynching. So I'll bet you'd be willing to strike a deal in order to save your ass."

"Go to hell," growled Beau.

"I might see you there someday, but it won't be today," declared Braun.

Beau stormed, "Listen, you sack of shit. You're the reason the other tug got captured and its crew killed. You didn't check the tow cable like a real captain would."

With that, Braun slammed his fist into the chin of Beau knocking him flat. Braun roughly picked him up, heaving Beau into a wooden kitchen chair and lashing his arms to the chair back with an electric cable he ripped from a nearby lamp. He then tied Beau's feet together and to the chair leg so he couldn't move.

Beau was groggy but still conscious.

"Ok, here's what's going to happen." warned Braun. "I'm sure you've got a wall safe here with a wad of cash just for a rainy day. You're going to point out where it is and give me the combination. Since I'm a reasonable man, I'll only take half of the cash and be on my way."

"Screw you," hissed Beau.

"I thought a southern gentleman like you would have a better attitude," mocked Braun, "but then I figured you're not much of a gentleman. So I came prepared to offer an alternative plan." With that Braun pulled a small flask that looked like a former pint whisky container out of his pants pocket. He put the flask on the kitchen table, then walked back to the front door where he had left a small duffle bag. He brought the duffle bag back with him.

Braun continued, "I brought a sample of that crude oil we gathered. I knew it would come in handy for a situation just like this. I also made up an indirect path flow container that takes about five minutes for this oil to pass through until it begins dripping out the bottom. I'm going to put this oil in the top and hang the container over your sorry-looking head. If you haven't given me the location and code to open your safe within five minutes, guess what? The oil will start dripping onto your bald head and within a couple of hours you'll be in so much pain from the virus that you'll beg me to shoot you. Of course, I'll be long gone by then."

Beau's kitchen had a beautiful hanging lamp centered over the kitchen table. Braun shoved the table out of the way and pushed Beau, still tightly bound to the chair, underneath the lamp. He pulled out his baffled container from the duffle bag. It resembled a clear glass gallon jug with a handle on the top. He hung his contraption on the light suddenly giving it an ominous glow.

"Ok, Mr. Calhoun," cajoled Braun. "It's your choice. Tell me where the safe is and its combination, or suffer an unimaginable death."

Beau licked his lips but didn't say a word, hoping Braun was bluffing.

Braun stepped up on one of the other chairs and carefully poured the tan colored liquid into the top of his special container. The top section was see-through glass with baffles built inside it. Braun positioned the container so Beau could just see it by looking up. The liquid slowly worked its way down around the baffles toward the bottom of the jug which had a hose-like opening on the end.

Beau was swallowing hard by the time the oil got about a quarter of the way down. Braun stood there with a "what do you think" look on his face.

"All right, you win," crooked Beau. "The safe is behind the farmland landscape painting in my den. The combination is CW25-CCW14-CW45- CCW3- CW36. Get me out from under this thing!"

"Come on, Mr. Calhoun." exclaimed Braun. "Do I look that dumb? I want to make sure the combination works and you really have something worthwhile. Then we'll see about giving you a pardon," Braun laughed cruelly.

While Braun had been waiting for Beau to reply, Beau was really testing the wire that roped his feet and hands. He felt given another couple of minutes he could free himself enough to rock the chair out from under the oil container. Besides, Beau was no pushover. He always had a plan, and this was no exception.

He actually had two safes. One that had his real money and one that was booby trapped. The latter was a five inch diameter tube about five feet deep with a 357 magnum pistol centered on a rigid mount near the back. The gun was on a visual recognition mechanism. If someone other than Beau peered into the safe, it would fire, hitting the offender between the eyes killing him instantly. If someone only reached in, a trip wire would also fire the weapon, most likely mutilating the arm and shoulder of the intruder. The entire system was strictly illegal, but that hadn't stopped Beau from having it installed.

The location and combination he gave Braun was for the booby-trapped safe. As Braun walked to the other room, he whistled "Taps" menacingly. With Braun out of the line of sight, Beau worked his hands and legs trying to gain some slack in the binding. To his dismay, the cord got tighter the more he moved. He admitted to himself that Braun was no amateur either. Beau began rocking the chair back and forth as best he could. It moved slightly but came to rest against the edge of the table and stopped. Beau was still slightly under the container discharge tube.

Suddenly, Braun's whistling stopped and Beau heard him say, "Aha! At least you're honest when your ass is on the line. Let's see what we've got in here."

What followed was an ear-shattering blast that shook the glassware in Beau's kitchen cabinets. The long tube in the safe actually magnified the gun's blast, making it twice as loud as it should have been. Beau then heard a dull thud which he figured was Braun's body hitting the floor. Beau laughed to himself, "I guess your "Taps" song wasn't for me after all."

Beau's smile quickly vanished from his face. He looked up and saw that the noise had shook the oil container so harshly that the poorly designed baffles collapsed, allowing the oil to flow more freely. The first drop nearly hit him in the eye. Several more hit his forehead. He screamed trying to rock the chair feverishly. It finally tipped sideways crashing him to the tile floor. He hit headfirst snapping his neck. Even in his death throes, he was still trying to slide away from the dripping oil. Beau's parting memory was of "Taps" sounding again, this time for him.

Chapter 53 - Lost Time

M anley Leeds was Beauregard Calhoun's personal doorman, butler, and general attendant and had been for nearly 30 years. Calhoun used to have a larger staff at his home. However, over the years they'd either left or he had gotten rid of them for various reasons, usually because Beau was just too hard to get along with. Leeds was the only one left, and one of the few people Calhoun truly trusted.

Leeds arrived at Calhoun's home at 8:30 AM with a bottle of Beau's favorite Bourbon Whiskey, Jack Daniels Black Label. Beau would ask Leeds to pick-up a fifth for him about every other week, but recently the order frequency had increased to every other day and this concerned Leeds. He had to walk a fine line between caring about Beau and keeping his job. Leeds made a mental note to talk to Beau about his health and mental state. Leeds knew Beau was depressed, but increasing alcohol consumption was definitely not the answer.

As Leed's inserted his key into the deadbolt, he was surprised to find it unlocked. "That's strange," he said to himself. "I know I locked this on the way out last night. I sure hope Mr. Calhoun didn't get so drunk he wondered outside and got lost." The Calhoun estate was pretty substantial with lots of thick woods and streams. Black bears, coyotes, and even some wolves were reported to have been spotted.

Leeds opened the door and headed down the hallway toward the kitchen. He knew right away the kitchen table was out of place as he could see the corner of it partially obstructing the doorway. Then he saw the soles of Beau's shoes and sprinted toward him, his breath catching in his throat. He yelled, "Beau, what have you done." As the scene registered in his mind Leeds stopped cold, shivers barreling down his spine. He rushed to the phone, nearly slipping on a greasy-like puddle on the floor. He shakily dialed 911.

The police were well aware who lived at the address and responded within less than fifteen minutes. Considering the secluded location of Calhoun's estate, a land speed record may have been tested. The police soon discovered Braun's body which had most of the jaw and forehead totally shattered. Apparently, Beau had loaded hollow point shells in the gun mounted in the booby-trapped safe. Dental records would be of no use in identifying this body.

The police got samples of the liquid on Beau's clothes and on the floor. Fortunately for the officers involved, they used crime scene gloves and did not contact the fluid.

An autopsy of Beau's body was conducted, and the cause of death was determined to be a skull fracture and broken neck. Unfortunately, an ongoing serial killer investigation had the local police department already working overtime. Even with Beau's stature and wealth, the town mayor wanted to look politically correct, and therefore put Beau's case at a lower priority. The fluid sample and stains on his clothes were deemed to be not significant, and due to delays and other priorities never got analyzed.

The investigation dragged on for months. Ultimately, the case was labeled a robbery/homicide. However, the identity of the intruder remained unknown. The case eventually landed in the "Cold Case" file.

Chapter 54 - Discovery Time

F or over three weeks medical research teams around the world were working feverishly to come up with a cure or at least a vaccine to combat the dreaded virus. Experiments had determined all higher level organisms, including mammals, reptiles, birds, insects, and fish, were susceptible to the virus. The death rate was 100%. Botanists got similar results with plant species.

Quinn and Bruce Langstrom from GG Oil were part of the team headed by Dr. Edwards. The team included several chemists from GG Oil as well as scientists from Berkeley and MIT.

The team gathered for their first team meeting. It was held in a small well-lit conference room adjacent to the various labs used for experiments. The conference room consisted of a long table surrounded by ten padded swivel arm chairs that rocked backwards. The room had a large periodic chart at the far end as well as numerous enlarged color photographs of successful test devices the lab team had designed in the past.

At their first team meeting Dr. Edwards's announced, "I am thinking our plan should be to first determine how the virus gets released from the crude oil. My thought is if we can establish that, it might lead us to a method to reverse the process, thus stopping the spread of the virus. Does anyone have any other thoughts or ideas? I'm open to all suggestions."

Amad Ramal, an MIT chemist from India, answered, "I think that's a good starting point. I'll contact the GG Oil chemical test manager to get the test protocol used on the crude oil samples mixed with the OxiMax dispersant. Supposedly the re-tests completed after Werner Strauss's death showed no issue. Yet he died from the virus. It just doesn't add up. Maybe there is something they missed."

"Great idea," replied Dr. Edwards. "Let's get this going ASAP. By the way, our schedule will be to have a brief team meeting in the morning to distribute any news from other teams and review the plan for the day. Then we'll have an end of day meeting to summarize any test results. I want to keep these meetings brief, no more than say thirty minutes. We need results, and sitting in meetings is time lost for getting real work done."

All team members appreciated Dr. Edwards' approach to problem solving. Keeping people informed was very important, but so was giving them the time needed to work the issues.

GG Oil was very cooperative, supplying the test protocol and samples of the OxiMax dispersant. Unfortunately, since Werner never had a chance to write a report on the initial testing, there was no way to compare the results of the original tests with the re-tests. Therefore, Ramal decided to repeat those re-tests, performing them exactly per the supplied test protocol. Unfortunately, after two days of extensive testing, the re-test results were confirmed.

Reporting at their next team meeting Ramal concluded, "We have been unable to cause a release of the virus. Scanni Electron Microscope (SEM) evaluation detected a gray-like crystalline molecule suspended within adjacent hydrocarbon molecules. This may be the virus, but it seems to remain inert, regardless of the concentration of OxiMax used."

Quinn, who had been listening throughout, spoke up, "Do you feel exposure time could be a factor?"

"Time certainly could be a variable, but we're assuming whatever caused the release of the virus must have occurred within about seven hours from when Werner's shift started and when his body was reported at about 11:00 PM. All bets are off concerning the long-term effects of the crude mixed with the OxiMax, but I don't think that's the immediate concern."

"I agree," responded Dr. Edwards.

Bruce Langstom asserted, "Dr. Edwards, we know that back before the Permian Period in geological history, the oxygen content in the earth's atmosphere was some 5% higher than it is today. Suppose somehow oxygen concentration increased momentarily around the crude oil when the dispersant was mixed in."

Dr. Edwards replied, "Like they say during brainstorming exercises, there are no bad ideas. Let's run some additional tests. I'd suggest bubbling oxygen-enriched air across some thin layers of the crude oil molecules."

Tests run the next day verified the theory. The higher levels of oxygen activated the gray parasite molecules which became the virus. The virus quickly consumed adjacent hydrocarbon molecules.

The team's end-of-the-day meeting concluded with Dr. Edwards urging, "Ok. Now we know increased oxygen is needed to unlock the molecular vault holding the virus prisoner. Trouble is we're missing how the hell the key gets to the lock. I challenge each of you to come up with some potential scenarios."

As they left the meeting Quinn pulled Bruce Langstrom aside and said, "Bruce, remember we had decided it would be a worthwhile exercise to review the photographs taken of the lab when Werner Strauss's body was found? Perhaps we can find evidence that might suggest something other than the test protocol had been used."

"Yeah, we had kind of put that on the back burner. It wouldn't hurt to have a look."

They pulled a copy of the police file supplied by GG Oil. There were well over a thousand photographs. Quinn and Bruce split them up and started the arduous task of sifting through them. After about twenty minutes Quinn spotted test tubes in a machine that looked out of place.

"Hey, Bruce, have a look at this," gestured Quinn excitedly. "What kind of machine is this?"

Remembering back to his college organic chemistry classes Langstrom answered, "That looks like a high-level shaker." He quickly confirmed that with Ramal.

"That type of machine is used to violently mix samples, right?" asked Quinn. "Extreme agitation is not part of the protocol, is it?"

"No, it's not," answered Langstrom. "Only mild mixing is specified." Looking more closely at the photograph, Langstrom added, "Let's computer enhance that picture. I see what could be markings on the test tubes."

Zooming in on the picture, Quinn extolled, "Bingo. Those are labels, and they read 'Crude/OxiM' with various percentage numbers beneath the title."

"Maybe violent mixing is the missing piece of the puzzle," suggested Langstrom. "Let's review this with Dr. Edwards."

After hearing their summation Dr. Edwards cheered, "Great work. I just got off the phone with the Pentagon. It turns out the OxiMax dispersant reacts with sea water giving off oxygen as a by-product. I'll bet a six pack that violent mixing breaks-up the crude oil sufficiently to bring the oxygen released by the dispersant in contact with the crude at close to a molecular level. That's what's needed to unlock the virus. Let's get testing started immediately."

Testing was resumed, this time with heavy agitation. The results left no doubt. A combination of crude oil from the Deep Horizon Well, OxiMax dispersant, and severe mixing caused the present calamity. They determined that waterspouts were present the afternoon the OxiMax was sprayed, which likely provided the needed extreme mixing. That was the good news.

Dr. Edwards relayed the bad news at the next team meeting. He declared, "Gentlemen, we all did a fantastic job establishing the series of events that got us into our present predicament. However, unfortunately we've come full circle because we just proved this is not a reversible process. I was hoping by figuring out the process we could stop the virus. It takes higher oxygen levels to release the virus; but once it becomes active, it apparently can survive at the present oxygen concentration in the atmosphere and in the ocean. I have a feeling reducing oxygen levels to some significantly lower level might stop the virus advance. Unfortunately, reducing oxygen levels on land or in large bodies of water is not a practical solution. Even if it could be done, all other life forms in that area would die as well. It's obvious to me that following this path will not lead to a useable answer."

Dr. Edwards continued, "At a recent team manager meeting, our team is being redirected. We are to focus on finding a method to determine whether the virus is present. To date, the only evidence we have on whether the virus exists in a given area is by life forms dying. If we're ever going to have a chance on eradicating this thing, we need to know the virus is present before it starts killing things. Other international teams are going to focus on a cure."

Dr. Edwards could tell by the group's reaction that this wasn't a particularly popular path. They all knew that the big kudos would come to the team that found the cure. So he added with a smile, "Of course, if we happen to find a potential antidote on the way to inventing a "virus present" test, we would certainly pursue that aggressively."

Chapter 55 - Marking Time

D r. Edwards's team accepted, although somewhat grudgingly, their new challenge of establishing a "virus present" test. In their first meeting after being reassigned, Dr. Edwards proposed, "I believe our top priority should be to come up with a relatively easy method to determine if the virus is present in water, both salt and fresh. Let's kick around some ideas."

There were several suggestions including a reverse osmosis process with an electronic monitor to detect the virus. However, all methods suggested involved complicated mechanisms for which neither designs or hardware existed.

"This may be a dumb idea," offered Quinn, "but suppose we try a litmus paper approach. As you all know, litmus paper is a crude but effective method for determining if a liquid is acidic or basic. Litmus paper, normally pale blue in color, turns red when placed in an acidic solution (pH less than 7.0), then turns back to pale blue when put in a basic solution (pH greater than 7.0)."

"My thought is to paint a tongue depressor type stick blue in color. Then, coat the painted surface with oxygen-enriched insoluble red blood plasma. When the stick is placed into water where the virus is present, the virus would consume the red plasma revealing the blue color below. If the virus is not present, the red-colored plasma remains."

Quinn looked around the meeting table, and to his surprise realized everyone was actually considering his idea.

Finally, Dr. Edwards responded, "As I said before, there are no dumb ideas. In fact, if it works, your approach would be both practical and inexpensive. Quinn, I want you and Bruce to work with Ramal on making up some sticks and testing them. The rest of us will pursue some of these more exotic ideas."

By the end of the day, Quinn, Bruce and Ramal had painted and coated the "Vitrus Sticks" as they called them. The group was too anxious to wait until morning, so stayed late to conduct test trials. They set up two beakers, one with fresh water and one with sea water. A second set of identical water-filled beakers was inseminated with the virus. The Vitrus Sticks were then immersed in the beakers. In the virus-free beakers, the Vitrus Sticks were still red after an hour. However, a different set of red-coated sticks turned blue after about ten minutes in the water containing the virus. This was a real breakthrough. After calling Dr. Edwards with the news, they all headed out for a hard- earned beer.

Chapter 56 - Bad Time

The group entered the morning meeting all smiles, expecting some congratulations. The mood was short lived. Dr. Edwards arrived about five minutes late, which was unusual for him. His look was somber.

Dr. Edwards opened the meeting by saying, "I'd like to congratulate Quinn, Bruce, and Ramal for establishing what appears to be a viable test method for verifying the presence of the virus, but I just received some bad news."

"I think we all are aware that other teams verified that temperatures above 800 degrees Fahrenheit killed the virus. Therefore, burning contaminated material was felt to be an adequate defense, at least on land. That's why back burns of the forest in the vicinity of the fish kill grave site were started immediately several weeks ago. The thought was that would form a dead zone through which the virus would have no means of spreading by contact."

"We just received reports that trees and birds are beginning to die outside the perimeter of that back burn. My fear all along has been what happens if the virus gets into the ground water, and even worse, what if it can survive evaporation? There could be horrifying repercussions. The virus could spread to open bodies of surface water via ground water, then, through normal evaporation, get dispersed over vast areas by normal rainfall."

"I bet I know what comes next," said Quinn. "Now that we have a "virus present" test, we need to determine if the virus can survive the evaporation/condensation cycle."

"Precisely," answered Dr. Edwards. "Plus, you'll get a chance to try out your Vitrus Sticks in the field. We've been requested to check Cody Lake and its supply stream. Cody is small, about one acre in area, and is the nearest to the fish kill burial site. Surveys show ground water flowing toward that lake. It's only about a half mile beyond the back-burn perimeter."

Quinn and Bruce set about making more Vitrus Sticks. Meanwhile, Ramal set up the equipment they'd need to conduct the evaporation experiments.

Ramal suggested, "Let's take the worse case. If the virus survives boiling water then rapid condensation, it surely will survive normal evaporation from streams and lakes." Everyone agreed.

Ramal set up distillation equipment in which they could boil samples of both fresh and saltwater. The vapor generated by boiling passed through chilled tubes which condensed the vapor, and the resulting fluid was collected in separate containers. Four test apparatuses were assembled, water installed, and the virus added to one each of the fresh and saltwater vessels. Vitrus Stick checks were made on each container. The sticks correctly identified the containers with the virus present.

After turning on the chilling flow, boiling of each of the samples commenced. Soon the condensed fluid began to appear in the collection containers. When sufficient condensate was accumulated, the fluid was checked with the Vitrus Sticks.

Ramal addressed the team at their end-of-the-day meeting. "The virus remains virulent, even after boiling and condensation. Now I'm downright scared that evaporation from surface water then condensation into rainfall, will spread the virus everywhere."

"I had a bad dream, or should I say nightmare, about this last night," sighed Dr. Edwards. "I woke up about 2:00 AM in a cold sweat. I put in an urgent call to a local hydrologist. He did some rough calculations, estimating it would take anywhere from two to three weeks for ground water to percolate from the fish burial site to the lake."

"Quinn and Bruce, please make up some more Vitrus Sticks and head out to Cody Lake as soon as you possibly can. I hope to hell we're not too late. If water with the virus has already reached the lake and started evaporating, we may already be doomed."

Everyone in the meeting room knew what this could mean. Quinn, always trying to be positive, voiced quietly, "It hasn't rained in over a week, and it's been cool and overcast with high humidity. So evaporation would be at a minimum. Maybe we'll finally catch a break." No one looked like they wanted to offer odds on that bet.

Chapter 57 - Prayer Time

It took well into the evening for Quinn, Bruce, and Ramal to make up the thirty Vitrus Sticks they felt they would need to test the water at Cody Lake and the small stream supplying it. Since it was already dark, they decided to wait until first thing in the morning to conduct the water evaluation.

Meanwhile, they reviewed maps and aerial photographs to formulate a test plan. They located a spring that supplied the stream that ultimately fed the lake. The stream, which seemed about only ten feet wide, meandered about 200 yards from the spring before emptying into the lake.

Bruce explained, "The underlying rock is limestone. Therefore, the groundwater probably follows a fairly contained path to the spring. That at least is positive since there shouldn't be a wide expanse of marshy area which might enhance evaporation."

Ramal offered, "I propose we split up. I'll start with the spring, and Bruce, you and Quinn check the stream at various points along its path to the lake. Depending on what we find, we'll then decide how much of the lake we need to check. We'd better bring along waders and a small boat.

Quinn added, "I have a 12-foot dingy I use for catching bait fish. We can take my truck and haul the boat and gear, no problem."

The morning dawned cool with a light breeze from the west. The trio was at the lake by 5:30AM, and the scene looked serene as the first rays of light sparkled across the lake. But it was dead quiet. The first call of morning birds and the last call of nighttime insects were nonexistent. Quinn commented, "Do you guys notice anything strange?"

"Yeah, it's eerily quiet," whispered Bruce.

"Stop the whispering," grumbled Ramal. "You're creeping me out."

As they approached the spring walking along the bank of the stream, they expected to hear the splash of a frog or see the tiny ripples from tadpoles or minnows breaking the water's surface. The stream was completely still as if it was totally sterile. As the sunlight began to brighten the scene, they also realized water lilies, that were usually prolific this time of year, were nonexistent, and grass and moss along the stream bank were brown and dying.

Quinn groaned, "This looks bad. We better make sure we don't contact the water or any of the plants along the stream." As they surveyed the area away from the stream, it appeared that the plants there were holding their own.

"When we leave," declared Bruce, "we better incinerate our boots and clothes to make sure we don't spread anything by contact."

"Hope we don't get arrested for driving back in the nude," quipped Quinn, hoping to lighten the mood.

They carried all their test equipment in a large duffle bag. Setting it down carefully, they pulled out the "Vitrus Sticks". Starting to pull out the sample bottles they brought, Ramal frowned, "Rather than getting samples and taking a chance of incorrectly identifying them, or worse, slicing a hole in our gloves with the pencil point, I'm thinking we should just dip the sticks in the water. If they don't change color in fifteen minutes, I think we can call the water acceptable. We can weight the sticks slightly with some fishing line and a stone so they don't float away. I'll work my way around this spring, and you guys work the stream."

Quinn slowly waded across the stream, which was only about ten feet wide, agreeing with the aerial photographs they had reviewed the previous evening. The stream was very slow moving, partially because of low rainfall during the last two months and partially because of the very gradual grade of the stream bed. In fact, looking down at the water, Quinn could not discern whether it was flowing or not.

Their plan was for Bruce to check the water on the east side of the stream while Quinn checked the west side. As Quinn plodded along the opposite bank, he nearly stepped on a dead bullfrog belly-up at the edge of the water. Looking closer, he noted dead minnows as well.

"Hey, Bruce," yelled Quinn. "I'm thinking we ought to save using the sticks in this area and move closer to the lake. I'm finding dead stuff along the bank here."

"So am I." replied Bruce. "Let's move south until we either get to the lake, or at least find plants along the bank that look like they're still alive."

Quinn nodded grimly.

They moved about 100 yards toward the lake where, to their relief, the stream banks suddenly turned green with mosses. Water lilies and pond grass also appeared sprouting from the stream bed.

Bruce hollered from the other side of the stream, "Quinn, I'm betting either the virus hasn't reached here yet, or it hasn't been here long enough to kill everything. Let's start testing about twenty yards upstream and then move twenty yards downstream from this location. I'll punch this spot into my hand held GPS so we can find it again. Let's call it the green zone."

After about an hour worth of testing, their intuition was verified. The Vitrus Sticks turned blue in ten minutes upstream of the green zone, but stayed red at the downstream location. They also tested at the green zone itself, and found that it took nearly an hour for the Vitrus Stick to turn blue. This suggested the virus was just now arriving there.

Ramal showed up just as they were documenting their results. "I hope you have better news than I do," challenged Ramal. "The virus is present around the entire circumference of the spring and at all depths."

"We have good news and bad," grumbled Quinn. "The virus is in the stream for the first 100 yards. There's a transition zone right here." Quinn pointed to a large rock he placed as a marker just in case the GPS failed. "The water is germ free from here, at least as far as we've tested."

"Okay. Let me get some measurements at the lake while you're finishing up," said Ramal.

Standing on the marking stone he'd just put in place, Quinn could get a better view of the stream. The difference from one direction to the other was startling. Looking south toward the lake looked like an oasis compared to the other direction. To the south the water looked crystal clear. He could see tadpoles and water spiders skittering across the surface and flying insects darting back and forth above. However, looking north toward the spring, the water was a steel gray whose banks and depths seemed barren as if poisoned with arsenic. Quinn took a deep breath, and muttered several obscenities to himself.

"Did you say something Quinn?" asked Bruce as he waded back across the stream.

"I'm just thinking out loud that if this spreads to the lake, we'll be in deep shit. We may have to evacuate the whole damn county or even the entire state."

Chapter 58 - Action Time

Ramal rejoined Quinn and Bruce. As they suspected, no evidence of the virus was found in the lake. They took their gear back to the truck and put their boots, clothes, and gloves into a plastic bag, sealing it tight.

As they headed back to the lab, Quinn had an idea. "Do you remember that Dr. Edwards mentioned a Japanese team found that formaldehyde kills the virus?"

"Kind of ironic, isn't it," voiced Bruce, "that formaldehyde, the same chemical used in embalming fluid, eliminates the virus. I mean, the stuff that kills the virus is the same stuff that preserves the bodies of the things the virus kills."

"Pretty profound thinker, isn't he?" goated Quinn while winking at Ramal.

"But what I'm thinking," said Quinn in a more serious tone, "is that we need to kill this here and now before it gets out of control. We don't need a two-front war both on land and sea. I say we shock the spring, stream, and lake with formaldehyde. We also should pump the fish kill burial site full of formaldehyde as well."

"You know that will environmentally ruin the entire area," cautioned Ramal. "It really is a pristine piece of land."

"Yes, I know, but the alternative of doing nothing will destroy so much more. It could wipe out the entire State of Louisiana or worse."

They all knew Quinn was right. "Let's give our recommendation at the-end-of-the-day meeting," declared Bruce. They hurried back to the lab.

When they arrived, the end of the day meeting was already in progress. All eyes looked to them as they entered the conference room. They nearly walked in with just their underwear on, but Quinn caught them, handing each a lab coat to cover up.

Ramal summarized the results of their testing at Cody Lake. He concluded with, "We think that there is a ray of hope if we can stop the virus before it reaches the lake. Quinn has suggested we shock the entire area, including the spring, stream, and lake as well as the fish kill grave with formaldehyde. We all concur with that recommendation."

"So do I," declared Dr. Edwards. "I'll call the executive director immediately after this meeting with a priority request this be started tomorrow. Excellent work by the way. My only additional request is that you guys repeat the water testing each week for the next three weeks. Let's pray that the formaldehyde shock works, and that the virus is gone by then."

All faces reflected the same heightened apprehension, realizing the severity of the situation.

Chapter 59 - Stress Time

Formaldehyde shocking of the Cody Lake area was begun the next day. With the land crisis temporarily on hold until next week's water testing, Dr. Edwards's team directed their attention to the more widespread and potentially much more dangerous ocean issue. They all were well aware that formaldehyde shocking would not work on a large scale body of water like the ocean. They needed something else and needed it soon.

The entire team realized they were battling a time constraint to contain the virus in the marine environment. However, no one was sure what the time boundaries were. Most scientists believed if the virus got to the waters of the Gulf Stream, not only the battle, but the war would be lost. The Gulf Stream current would transport the virus throughout the Atlantic Basin, and weather patterns would ultimately distribute it to all parts of the globe. Most felt they had less than a month before the virus reached this underwater highway, and that was without considering the impact of rainfall.

Quinn began taking divers out to reefs in the area on a daily basis to survey the situation and try to establish a perimeter. However, conditions were worsening on each trip. The only positive thus far was that Vitrus Stick checks of the ocean surface in the vicinity of the dissipated Logan Slick showed no evidence of the virus. This suggested that the spread of the virus via evaporation and rainfall might be minimized.

However, they did find that starting at depths of 100 feet and below, the virus seemed to be proliferating. In their team meeting Dr. Edwards theorized, "My thought is as the virus consumes plankton and other drifting type microscopic creatures, it becomes denser, gradually descending toward the bottom. It then attacks the reef and its associated ecology, or sea grass if no coral outcroppings exist. Any ideas on how we can verify that?"

Quinn offered, "Perhaps we should perform a night dive. Sometimes the marine environment takes on a different perspective when viewed at night. Maybe we can see something we'd otherwise miss in the daylight."

"Let's do it," replied Dr. Edwards anxiously. "We desperately need a breakthrough. Maybe finding out what's going on out there will provide a hint on how to proceed."

That evening Quinn and five other divers prepared their gear for the night dive. They each included a helmet-mounted light. Quinn proposed, "My thought is to head toward "Jadarns Reef". Don't bother asking because, no one seems to know the origin of the name."

"But anyway, as of yesterday it seemed to be unaffected by the virus. However, it is only about 100 yards from an outcropping that showed signs of stress. It's at a depth of about 140 feet with basically no current to worry about. I suggest we anchor about 20 yards from Jadarns, descend to 120 feet, then turn off our lights. Hopefully, we'll see something worth reporting." All hands agreed to the plan.

*****

They reached their destination, dropping anchor at 9PM. It was a humid, dead calm, moonless night with an occasional flicker of heat lightning in the distance. The water was an inky black as it slapped gently on the side of the boat. Usually the boat's lights would attract flying fish, but that was not the case tonight.

As they dropped one by one into the water, Quinn thought he saw some faint light below, but attributed it to a reflection from one of the other diver's helmet lamps. Staying close together in a group, they gradually descended to the agreed on depth. When they arrived at the predetermined location, Quinn verified it with his depth gauge then signaled to the others to kill their lights.

The result proved downright frightening. He could sense all of them gasping from fright. To their astonishment, they were greeted with what appeared to be one-half inch teardrop shaped globules that faintly pulsed with a green ominous glow.

These globules drifted downward toward the reef, almost like heavy, damp snowflakes in a windless winter night. Some had already reached the highest coral formations, oozing slowly over their branches and dripping to the formations below. It would have been a breathtakingly beautiful scene if they didn't already know what soon would follow.

Quinn uttered, "God Help Us" silently to himself. He motioned to the diver tasked with filming videos to start his camera to record the morbid spectacle for posterity. As soon as they surfaced Quinn forwarded the videos electronically to Dr. Edwards. He also sent them to Grace to show on TV as evidence of rapidly deteriorating conditions. Quinn felt everyone must know the severity of the situation.

Chapter 60 - Test Time

D r. Edwards called the team together for a special meeting. They all had been working twelve-hour days seven days a week. The stress was taking its toll. Dr. Edwards spoke tiredly, "Our team has been re-directed again. All teams have been placed in emergency mode. We have to find a way to stop the virus advance in the ocean or the consensus is we're all condemned."

"None of the teams nationally or internationally have had any success finding a cure or vaccine to protect against the virus. The only positive thing learned is that the virus only survives about one week without living organisms to feed on."

"I implore you all to wrack your brains for any possible solution. Leave no stones unturned. Our very lives depend on it."

*****

On the morning of July 7th Quinn had a thought and decided to touch base with Langstrom for his opinion. Quinn got to the point immediately, "Since so far all available attempts have had no positive effect on combating the virus, I was thinking maybe a different approach is needed. What if we reviewed the species that geology shows survived the mass extinction? Perhaps present-day species are close enough to their ancestors that we could somehow extract or develop a cure from them."

Langstrom liked the idea saying, "Quinn you just might have something." They spoke with Dr. Edwards who enthusiastically endorsed the idea.

Quinn and Langstrom grabbed their laptop computers and met to review geological history. They decided to review the marine ecology since this was where they needed answers immediately. It became obvious as they conducted their research that the extinction rate of marine organisms was catastrophic. Most marine invertebrate genera registered from 96% to 100% extinct. The only exceptions were the bivalves, such as clams, mussels, and scallops, and the ostracodes (small crustaceans). Extinctions in these Genera approached 60%.

Langstrom felt pursuing a cure from the ostracodes was futile, given their small size of several millimeters or less. The bivalves, however, held merit, although where to start would require much more expertise than either of them had.

However, Quinn came up with two other creatures showing promise due to their ancestry dating back prior to the mass extinction. They were the Horseshoe Crab and the Sea Anemone. Fossils showed that the earliest horseshoe crab species were crawling around shallow coastal seas at least 100 million years before the mass extinction. Plus, extracts from horseshoe crab blood is presently used to test for the purity of medicines and medical equipment. So at least this was available in limited quantities, perhaps providing a starting point for testing.

Sea Anemones had potential due to their ability to produce neurotoxins. Although neither Quinn nor Langstrom saw where this ability might be useful, they didn't want to eliminate the possibility. After an exhaustive day of research, they decided to present what they found to Dr. Edwards.

Dr. Edwards was encouraged by their findings. As he put it,

"their ideas were utilizing known natural defenses to combat an invasive enemy that these specific creatures had survived before."

Woods Hole Oceanographic Institute was the largest research facility that regularly extracted horseshoe crab blood for use in the medical field. Quinn and Langstrom called and the Woods Hole team was anxious to help. They agreed to send one of their top researchers, a man named Bart Rada, with 16 ounces of horseshoe crab blood to Dr. Edward's labs which were now set up at MIT.

Quinn, Langstrom, and Rada formed an immediate bond and made a great team. Working together they tried to figure a way to utilize the horseshoe crab blood. The blood is copper based, unlike mammal blood which is iron based. The copper base gave the crab blood an eerie blue coloration.

They initiated testing, coating small fish with the blood then introducing the virus into the water. They quickly found that the blood was effective in repelling the virus. However the blue blood soon washed off, and the virus would move in and consume the host.

They knew they had to determine a method to keep the crab blood on the subject long enough to force the virus to "starve to death". Of course there was also the matter of dispensing the blood over a large area, but they were not even close to having to worry about that yet.

Again, Quinn came through with an idea. In their morning meeting Quinn commented, "As I understand it, the mucus in clams and oysters transports the food ingested by the creature to its stomach. Way back in history, the clams ancestor's mucus must somehow have either repelled or destroyed the virus in organisms the clam was eating such that it did not harm the clam itself. Mucus is sticky. Perhaps we could mix the horseshoe crab blood with clam mucus and keep the mixture in place on our subject."

Both Langstrom and Rada starred at Quinn in amazement. "Let's try it," they both said in unison.

Finding sufficient live clams and extracting the mucus proved a challenge, but here Rada's expertise and contacts were invaluable. Using miniature syringes, they were able to extract small quantities from each specimen without killing the subject. After numerous attempts at mixing the mucus with the crab blood, they finally came up with a consistency that seemed to provide enough adhesion to justify testing.

For this test they introduced a small cloud of the mucus/crab blood mixture into a small tube of water, and then forced their test fish to swim through it. All three cheered when the fish exited the tube into its tank with a distinctive blue coloration. But the real success occurred when the virus was introduced into the tank. The fish survived five days. Unfortunately, the virus survived as well and ultimately destroyed the fish. However, subsequent tests found that by reapplying the mixture, a creature could outlast the virus.

This was an astonishing breakthrough. However, the odds of this working anywhere outside of the laboratory environment seemed a long shot at best. What they really needed was something that could kill the virus as it was being repelled from the area by their crab blood/clam mucus mixture.

This time Rada had a tantalizing suggestion. Rada described, "The Sea Anemone utilizes a toxin that is actually a mix of neurotoxins. The toxin not only can kill its prey, but also when released in the water can act as a repellant against potential predators. We don't fully understand how they work, but perhaps we could add this toxin in a diluted amount sufficient to kill the virus but not strong enough to be harmful to other creatures."

Extracting the toxin from Sea Anemones had been done at Woods Institute, and small quantities were available. Finding the correct dilution proved tricky, but tests finally came up with a concentration that seemed to work. They were able to get at least one fish to outlast the virus. After two days in the special tank with the deadly microbe, the fish, although sluggish, was still alive. There was no evidence of the virus.

The team had no idea whether their antidote would work on plants or other sea creatures, but they were running out of time. A separate team tried the mixture on various sea plants and it seemed to work. However, there just wasn't enough time to complete comprehensive tests on all sea life. There was also a serious concern of how to manufacture sufficient quantities of the mixture and how to dispense it in the ocean.

*****

The team gave their results to Dr. Edwards, who then contacted pharmaceutical companies via the internet with an urgent plea for help. Grace and her news team had engaged people and companies world wide, generating intense interest as people realized this was a global menace that in reality could destroy life on earth.

Both military and civilian entities began mobilizing to supply ships, pumping rigs, and nozzles to dispense clouds of the mixture while others worked out man-made chemical formulas to replicate the natural materials produced by the horseshoe crabs, clams, and sea anemones. It turned out the military had experimented on a synthesized neurotoxin based on the sea anemone's toxin, so that piece of the puzzle was already available.

Meanwhile, oceanographers worked up maps of tides and currents in the contaminated areas. The plan being proposed was to attempt an underwater "backburn" using the "Quinnstrom" mixture, which had been named after Quinn and Langstrom who had come up with the formula. The hope was it would force the virus into a smaller and smaller area of the ocean. They would then shock that area with a more concentrated form of the sea anemone toxin to destroy the virus.

On paper this looked possible, but logistically it was a nightmare. There were so many things that had to come together at the same time. Would the man-made formulation be as potent as the mixture made from the natural creature produced components? Could the pumps disperse it in the correct concentration and in the desired locations? Would the current and other weather predictions be accurate enough? What ocean depth coverage was acceptable? The more experts discussed the potential scenarios, the more the odds of success diminished. They estimated they had two weeks to set the plan, whatever the final one was, in motion.

Chapter 61 - The Shinning Light

As their D-Day approached, the ocean spraying plan was finalized. Ships, pumping equipment, and crews were mobilized at ports closest to the "back-burn" area. Bulk quantities of the Quinnstrom chemical mixture were produced and hastily distributed to each of the ships.

However, two days before ocean spraying was to commence, Grace got an unusual request from a most unlikely source. Grace now had a team of over ten people working for her, including a secretary and two staffers answering phones.

Her secretary, Ginger Adams, came to her about 9:00 AM with a strange, questioning look on her face. Ginger stated, "Grace, a man claiming to be Dr. Masaru Emoto would like to speak to you. He says he is the President Emeritus of the International Water for Life Foundation. He wants to propose some sort of prayer for the water campaign."

Grace's initial reaction was, "That's all we need, some sort of crackpot Bible thumper advocating a moratorium to stop ocean spraying." But something deep inside her mind nagged at her. She had a strange inner feeling that she should speak to him.

"Ok, Ginger. Put him through to me," Grace whispered. Ginger cocked her head with an "are you kidding" look on her face. They were all working nearly 20 hours per day since the search for a virus cure had began, and she figured no way would Grace have even a minute or two for this.

"Are you sure?" asked Ginger.

Grace nodded yes.

"I'll put him through," responded Ginger shaking her head warily.

Grace put the call on speaker and answered, "Good morning, this is Grace Connelly."

After a brief pause, a pleasant voice with a noticeable oriental accent replied, "Good morning this is Dr. Emoto. I and my students have been following your reports on the oil spill and resulting microbe release. We are deeply concerned."

"We all have that same feeling," responded Grace. "In fact, we are very fearful for life in general." Grace noted a detectable static on the line and a seeming delay in conversation responses.

Grace added, "Dr. Emoto you sound like you are far away. Where are you calling from?"

After a few seconds a reply came, "I am calling from Yokohama, Japan."

Grace hesitated a moment, trying to recall where she had heard the name. She was drawing a blank. She finally answered, somewhat embarrassed for not being better informed, "What can I do for you sir?"

Dr. Emoto commented, "I sense you are struggling with who I am. I have authored several books including 'Messages from Water' and 'The True Power of Water'. Have you read them by chance?"

Grace made a vague connection in the back of her mind and answered, "I have heard of your books, but I must admit I have not read them." Something inside her jabbed at her mind wishing she had.

"I believe strongly," continued Dr. Emoto, "in the power of words and focused prayer. In our country we practice Hado. Hado creates words. Words are the vibrations of nature. Therefore, beautiful words create beautiful nature and ugly words create ugly nature. This is the root of the universe. I have shown that human thoughts and feelings can affect physical reality."

Grace was almost mesmerized by Dr. Emoto's words. Then her consciousness was jolted by a memory. She added excitedly, "Didn't a few years back you publicize your experiments on ice crystals where positive thoughts produced a definite change in the condition of the water?"

"Yes, that's correct," replied Dr. Emoto. "In fact, similar tests were conducted on rice and other plants where positive words produced healthy plants and negative words reduced the plant's growth."

"What I am proposing," continued Dr. Emoto, "is that you go on your daily televised news update asking that people all over the world say a simple prayer at the same time. Where possible, people should face the ocean when saying the verse. Any body of water or even a glass of water would be helpful if the ocean is not accessible. Perhaps an e-mail campaign would help get the word out concerning the date and time for the prayer."

Grace was not a particularly religious minded person. In fact, she hadn't been to church since last Easter, but for some reason she felt an inspiration that nearly overwhelmed her. She knew this was something that must be done.

"Dr. Emoto," breathed Grace, "thank you so much for your thoughts and concern. Please help me formulate the prayer. I will go worldwide with a plea for all people to say this prayer together at 6:00 PM two days from now. This will coincide with commencement of ocean spraying."

Dr. Emoto had several suggestions for Grace but wanted her to put it in her own words. After thanking Dr. Emoto, Grace contacted Luther, figuring since he was a former Chaplin in the Marines, he could contribute to the final verse. Luther had heard of Dr. Emoto and loved the idea. Based on Dr. Emoto's input, Grace and Luther came up with this simple prayer:

> *"To all living creatures in the Gulf of Mexico, mankind is sorry for unleashing this virus in our world. Please forgive us. Thank you. We love you."*
>
> *"To the oil virus, you are a fool for trying to destroy life in our beautiful world. Perhaps it was necessary millions of years ago, but it is not today. Go back to the bowels of the earth and do not return."*

Grace went live an hour after her discussion with Dr. Emoto. She delivered such a heart-felt message that even her hardboiled editor had tears in his eyes. All the nightly newscasts worldwide picked up on the story and replayed the plea for a united prayer. Soon millions of e-mails, text messages, and tweets buzzed through cyberspace. Not since Apollo 13's miraculous in-space disaster, did the world seem to acknowledge and act on the need for a united prayer. It was not known accurately how many said the prayer at 6:00 PM on August 8, 2010, but the estimate was in the hundreds of millions with many facing the ocean to recite the words.

Chapter 62 - August 8, 2010 – Salvation

The ocean spraying commenced as planned. Over a thousand ships were pressed into service. As expected, there were some incidences, such as failed pumps and clogged nozzles, but overall the spraying campaign went well.

By design the Quinnstrom mixture was delivered at two depths, 10 feet and 50 feet from the ocean bottom. Ships started in an area where reefs were healthy, then moved toward the infected areas. They covered an ocean area of five nautical miles in a coordinated pattern hoping to either kill the virus outright or push it toward a centralized location where minimal reef and sea grass beds existed. A more concentrated toxin would be sprayed there if needed. The entire process was to be repeated in five days.

Vitrus Stick checks and water analysis completed prior to the spraying showed virulent virus at each infected reef and sea grass zone, and plankton voids in between each zone. The voids suggested the virus had destroyed all waterborne life in those areas.

Prior to the second spraying, Vitrus Stick checks and water samples were again taken. A ray of hope glimmered. The Vitrus Sticks took longer to change color, suggesting the virus was weakening. The voids were still present, but the edges of the void areas seemed to show evidence that plankton was returning. Of some concern, however, was the fact that the centralized location showed no evidence of the virus.

Grace again pleaded on national news for a second prayer session coinciding with the start of the second phase of spraying. Again, hundreds of millions responded repeating the prayer with heart-felt enthusiasm.

Chapter 63 - August 16, 2010

Three days after the second spraying, analysis showed no signs of the virus. TV news flashed the reports. Grace tried to contain her excitement since scientists felt follow-up water testing was needed over several weeks before claiming success. However, there was no doubt that the results were positive. Also, the land-based water tests at Cody Lake proclaimed virus free results.

*****

A few days later the Tidal Surge Group was asked to assemble to receive a message from the President of the United States. The President thanked them in person, and presented them with the highest civilian honor achievable.

When the President asked whether there was anything he could do for them, to everyone's surprise, Quinn stood and noted, "Would it be possible to have the dissected cat's remains returned to me. I promised her owner that I would return them to her for proper burial." The President answered with genuine compassion that he would have Homeland Security Director Oman retrieve the remains.

The following week Quinn received a special delivery package with a return address labeled "The White House". After removing the crisp wrapping, Quinn found a small beautifully decorated sealed coffin with a perfectly sized United States flag draped over it. It was a miniature replica of what would be used for military funerals. A small granite tombstone was included emblazoned with gold letters that read:

Herein Lies Chrissy. Her Sacrifice Saved the Lives of Millions. Her Life Was Not Lost In Vain. God Bless All Creatures.

The next morning Quinn and Grace drove out to the Trudeau's place. Mrs. Trudeau met Quinn at the door. Flinging her thin, withered arms around him she said, "I heard on last night's news that President Obama had personally requested a special burial package for Chrissy. Quinton, it makes my tired heart sing knowing there are still people who keep their word. Thank you so much for remembering your promise."

"Mrs. Trudeau," replied Quinn, "Chrissy played a significant role in cracking the mystery and potentially saving millions of lives. We all owe both you and Chrissy a huge debt of gratitude."

With that, Quinn dug a grave in a shady location that Mrs. Trudeau had specially selected. They placed the presidential-designed coffin in the ground, then took turns shoveling in the dirt. Quinn set the tombstone in place and Mrs. Trudeau placed a bouquet of flowers she'd picked from her yard alongside the grave. She said a prayer in Cajun. Although that concluded the ceremony, the tears flowed freely for many minutes.

Grace made her final televised news conference on the virus status at 12:00 PM. She closed the newscast with pictures she'd taken of Chrissy's burial along with a solemn commentary on how fortunate mankind was that this would not be repeated millions of times.

*****

A month later the Tidal Surge group met for the last time. Champagne was passed around and a hearty toast delivered, giving thanks to all involved. The Primordial Tide had been turned, the virus eradicated.

Quinn closed the meeting saying, "I don't really know whether the spraying or the millions of prayers defeated this plague. Perhaps both together turned the dreaded Primordial Tide. The only thing I do know is it worked and I give thanks for that blessing."

Epilogue

E milio Gomez – Is a person that no one still alive at the
conclusion of the story knew existed. Emilio was a hard
working, deeply religious, family man. He had been away from
his wife and two-month-old son for nearly 2 years. When he left
Guatemala two years ago for the United States, he promised his wife
and family he would return with enough money to get their son the
medical care he desperately needed.

Emilio entered the United States illegally, but stood out from
many others in the same situation by his nautical skills and dedicated
work ethic. He never watched TV news because it depressed him.
Instead, he listened to classical music and wrote detailed letters to
his family. He had a goal of saving $50,000. $20,000 was required to
provide the operation his son needed. The other $30,000 would give
him and his family a comfortable life in the hills near his hometown
of Sabrano, Guatemala. His plan was to buy a farm there, and raise
a family based on hard work and devotion to God.

Emilio was well on his way to achieving his goal when he met
Captain Braun. The wages he would make crewing on Braun's tug
would not only put him over his goal but also achieve it sooner than
he had dreamed possible. He had no idea that their mission was both
dangerous and illegal.

He signed on and worked precisely to the Captain's orders. They completed their contract to the letter. Captain Braun paid Emilio his wages and added a bonus the evening after they had grounded the oil-filled barge and sailed the tug to the ship salvage yard.

The next morning Emilio headed for Guatemala. He never looked back. He never heard the news about the virus or even the plea for prayer. He certainly would have prayed for he was a devoted Catholic. Even worse, Emilio had no idea he ultimately was the only living person that knew of the existence and location of a barge full of drums containing crude oil with the deadliest virus that had ever existed on Earth. The virus could last indefinitely. However, the oil drums themselves were a different story. They had a limited life, especially when subjected to the brackish water and humid, sun drenched environment of the bayou.

Although this oil had been sprayed with the OxiMax dispersant, it may not have been violently mixed. The water spouts may not have contacted the portion of the slick from which it was siphoned. However, no one knew what impact long exposure to the environment might have on the crude oil/dispersant mixture. Would the virus remain fatal? Or could other life forms develop over years of exposure if the virus laced oil was released gradually into the isolated, bayou environment?

Only time and fate would tell.